Everything
Beautiful
in the
World

LISA LEVCHUK

Everything
Beautiful
in the
World

FARRAR STRAUS GIROUX
NEW YORK

For my parents

Copyright © 2008 by Lisa Levchuk
All rights reserved
Distributed in Canada by Douglas & McIntyre Ltd.
Printed in the United States of America
Designed by Jay Colvin
First edition, 2008
1   3   5   7   9   10   8   6   4   2

www.fsgkidsbooks.com

Library of Congress Cataloging-in-Publication Data
Levchuk, Lisa.
    Everything beautiful in the world / Lisa Levchuk.— 1st ed.
        p.   cm.
    Summary: Toward the end of the disco era, seventeen-year-old Edna refuses to
visit her mother, who is in a New York City hospital undergoing cancer treatment,
and barely speaks to her father, who finally puts her in psychotherapy, while her
crush on an art teacher turns into a full-blown affair.
    ISBN-13: 978-0-374-32238-0
    ISBN-10: 0-374-32238-4
    [1. Coming of age—Fiction.   2. Family life—New Jersey—Fiction.
3. Teachers—Fiction.   4. Cancer—Fiction.   5. Psychotherapy—Fiction.
6. High schools—Fiction.   7. Schools—Fiction.   8. New Jersey—History—
20th century—Fiction.]   I. Title.

PZ7.L572313Eve 2008
[Fic]—dc22

2007016603

Everything
Beautiful
in the
World

Me

I AM SEVENTEEN YEARS OLD and my mother who might be dying always says I am the center of the universe. She says that everything in the world revolves around me, but I disagree. Lately I feel like an astronaut out on a space walk—constantly praying the tube attaching me to the ship doesn't snap and send me flying into outer darkness.

The Fight

THIS SPACE-WALK FEELING started intensifying in March, about a month after my seventeenth birthday. I'd been looking forward to my birthday for at least a year because on that day I would finally get my driver's license. But good things usually have a downside, and as it turned out, getting my license meant my mother and I were fighting even more than usual. After she got my most recent report card in the mail, she refused to let me drive at all unless it was absolutely necessary. She's right about my grades. They aren't all that hot.

It's my junior year, and according to my mother, the grades I get this year will determine my entire future as it relates to college. On this particular night, my mother was trying to force me to miss what I thought was going to be an extremely fun party. Word was that there was going to be live music and that college kids were going to be there. My mother wanted to call the *parents*, for God's sake. I knew the parents were going away for the weekend, so I kept accusing her of not trusting me, trying to guilt-trip her into letting me go. Though I don't know a lot about her teenage years, my sense is my mother was a bit of a Goody Two-shoes and that she doesn't really get how much times have changed. She told me I wasn't going to run around with what she called "the jet set," which was an old-fashioned way of saying I wasn't going to hang out with cool people. In my defense, it did feel like she was trying to ruin any chance I had for a normal social life.

Just as we were arriving at the most heated part of the fight, the phone rang. My mother glared at me, put down her dishcloth, and answered. She listened and then laughed a weird laugh, not her normal laugh. She laughed her spooky laugh and said a few more words I couldn't quite follow.

"Fights are postponed," she said as she hung up.

Why? I was too scared to ask.

Before she answered that phone, I had said something almost unforgivable to her. She was riding me pretty hard about getting out of control and I came back with a nasty comment. I was waiting for her to say something equally mean or even slap me, but all I got was "Fights are postponed." This was worse than a slap because you can't *postpone* a fight. Postponing a fight means that it ends without ever being over. And if it ends at the worst possible moment, that's it. No more fighting. I was winning, but then I lost. My mother was just about to let me have it, and then she didn't. The next thing I knew, she was in the hospital being operated on for cancer that had spread through her lymph nodes.

The truth is we'd been fighting quite a bit since September. For one thing, it felt like she was exhausted and cranky all the time. One day around Thanksgiving I came home from school and she was asleep on the couch with her full-length down coat and shoes on. She woke up, but she didn't explain why she would do something so strange. At the same time, I was being even more elusive about my life than I usually am.

I study other families whenever I get the chance to see if mine fits the mold. My parents are certainly correct about the fact that I don't like filling them in on how I feel or what I'm doing, but isn't that normal? The trouble is I started clamming up earlier than most kids. I don't know why I stopped telling them about my life. Even when you think you understand the reasons you are doing something, I've discovered you can be dead wrong about your *own* motives. Somewhere along the way, I got the impression my parents didn't necessarily want or need to know about the bad parts of my life. Most of the really weird stuff, like the misinformation I got about sex (i.e., thinking in fourth grade you could get pregnant by rubbing your rear end against the rear end of a boy), I've worked through on my own. Still, I was definitely a spooky kid. How many preschoolers are afraid of the birds on the wallpaper in the hallway? How many second-graders still have an invisible friend and are consumed with the fear of death? I'm not sure elementary school children are supposed to be complete hypochondriacs. But there it is.

My father is pissed because I haven't been to the hospital since the day we took my mother in, which was March 13, an unlucky day if you ask me. I've even begun to go so far as to get into the shower when the phone rings so I can't talk to my mother when she calls. If no one is home, I stand there pretending to be invisible. I will admit my behavior is not exactly normal, but I have reasons for not wanting to see her, reasons that go beyond the lousy thing I said to her, but those reasons would be tough to explain. If it weren't for Mr. Howland, I don't know how I'd get through any of this.

Mr. Howland

THE ONLY THING that distinguishes Mr. Howland's classroom from all others is the presence of Mr. Howland. He teaches Sculpture, Ceramics, and Art History, so the arrangement of the tables in the room can change depending on what class was just being taught. I'm in his fourth-period Ceramics class, having taken Sculpture in the fall. I won't try to lie to you and say that I have any talent; in fact, I am very close to the bottom of the class in terms of artistic gifts. Our most recent project was to make a simple, functional mug. After spending what felt like hours working to get the clay centered on the wheel, I got sick of trying and let my mug be lopsided. Its functionality was further hindered by the fact that the handle broke off in the kiln. Mr. Howland teased me good-naturedly about it, but there was no way to disguise the fact that my mug was a disaster. It looked quite a bit like the one made by the mainstreamed student, Tyrone Love. Tyrone spent about two weeks rolling the clay into a ball and didn't even try to give it a form (Tyrone doesn't use the wheel) until right before the due date. So his mug was pretty dysfunctional as well.

There are about nine kids in ceramics because the school could afford to purchase only one potter's wheel. Of the six girls, I would have to say five of us are there strictly for Mr. Howland. He's got sandy blond hair that always looks tousled in a cute just-got-out-of-bed way. Aside from his never-combed-yet-stylish hair, he wears horn-rimmed glasses that would most likely look stupid on someone else, but he makes them cool. Mr. Howland told us about the prep school in Virginia he attended where you had to wear a coat and tie every day, and it is very appealing that he still has a preppy style. He could easily star as Jay Gatsby in a movie of *The Great Gatsby*. Lest I forget, his khaki pants are always a bit too loose, leaving what my friend Patty and I call the "sweet sag" in the back. His butt is quite flat, and both Patty and I find that attractive. Mr. Howland can sculpt, paint, and make a perfectly shaped ceramic bowl any time he feels like it. He has a small office in the front of his classroom, and the girls joke about him being some kind of superhero who changes into a new identity when he shuts the door. In addition to all of his other gifts, he is an expert in art history, a film buff, *and* he lets us listen to music during class. Basically, we are all madly in love with him.

The first time I ever saw him outside of school was when I was shopping in Foodtown with my mother during the summer. He passed us in the produce aisle, his shopping cart filled with healthy-looking vegetables. I didn't really know him, but I waved. There is a rumor he used to teach at a pretty swanky boarding school in Connecticut, but he left that job for reasons no one knows. Seems like downward mobility to me, but I'm glad he ended up here. We didn't even *have* ceramics or art history until he showed up. As I said, we passed him and I waved. I knew he was a teacher, and I knew a lot of girls had crushes on him.

"Who is that handsome man you waved to?" my mother asked.

"A teacher in my school," I told her.

Though I don't see eye to eye with her on many things, there was something about my mother finding Mr. Howland handsome that made me think he was the best-looking guy in the world. Despite my lack of artistic talent, I decided to pick up his Sculpture class in the fall. Now, like everyone else, I look forward to Mr. Howland's class for most of the day and feel a sense of loss when the bell rings at the end of the period. Even other teachers are attracted to him. Patty, one of the best students in school, gets to have him over to her house sometimes. Her mother is chairman of the English Department, and though Patty's mom is much older than Mr. Howland and his wife, she invites them over for dinner and is actually friends with them. Sad to admit it, but I found myself cultivating a closer friendship with Patty after I learned how close her mother was with the Howlands. Patty's mom stops by Ceramics class occasionally, and it sometimes feels like she is trying to flirt and be sexy, but the combination of her age and a serious-sounding smoker's cough makes me doubt Mr. Howland finds her overly desirable.

What I like best about Mr. Howland is the way he makes you believe your project is beautiful even when it is lopsided and missing the handle. He has a way of holding you in his sphere of attention that is really powerful. Throughout the fall, I was very quiet because I am not the kind of person who likes to talk unless I'm comfortable. I made some passable sculptures and was content to catch a smile or two from Mr. Howland. The first time I noticed he was paying attention to me was right before Christmas vacation when the head fell off my sculpture. I was quite upset, because I had really put in effort and even named my figure Uncle Benny, after my favorite uncle. Mr. Howland gave me a pep talk about how all artists suffer losses. He actually referred to me as an *artist*, which is a total laugh, but I felt like Georgia O'Keeffe or someone when he said it. He looked into my eyes in a way that made my knees go numb.

This might sound completely crazy, but I am going to admit something pretty strange. I knew very early on that Mr. Howland would end up being an important person in my life. I know it sounds totally unbelievable and impossible given the fact that he is a married teacher and I am his student, but as far back as that day in Foodtown, I saw Mr. Howland as someone who was going to play a role in my fate—my *destiny*, even. This is not as strange as you might think: when we were kids, my best friend, Barbie, and I used to make up and record soap operas on a tape recorder, and my characters were always having affairs. When I was in elementary school, I was madly in love with Frank Ryan, a cop from the show *Ryan's Hope* who must have been about thirty years old. Frank was married to a mentally unstable woman named Delia, but his true love was Jillian Coleridge. Even then there was something I loved about older men, something about how they look cute in a sad way. I've had a few boyfriends, none of them really serious, but I've never felt about any of them the way I do about Mr. Howland.

I'm not saying he noticed me right away, because he did not. It was well after Thanksgiving before he started laughing at my jokes and listening when I told stories. But back in December, right after Uncle Benny's head fell off, I knew that my instincts had been correct. The look Mr. Howland gave me while he consoled me led me to believe that something more could follow. In Latin class, Ms. Clewell makes us write the phrase *Alea jacta est* at the top of the page when we take a test. Those words, "The die is cast," are the words, she told us, that Caesar said in 49 B.C. right after making the momentous decision to cross the Rubicon and forever change the history of Rome. When Mr. Howland stared into my eyes and held my gaze, the words *alea jacta est* popped into my mind. I knew he was making a decision. At the time, I couldn't have told you with certainty what would come or how we would change the future, but the die was definitely cast.

Mr. Howland is the only person I've talked to about my mother's sickness. I probably wouldn't even have told *him*, but my emotions forced my hand. It was the day after we took her to the hospital. I was massacring another lump of clay on the wheel. Mr. Howland was being patient but, at the same time, getting frustrated with me. One second I was sitting at the wheel laughing and the next I had tears streaming down my face. Mr. Howland didn't say a word; he pretended I was fine. But after class, he let me sit in his office and I blurted out how my mother was sick. He listened to the entire story, even the part where we were fighting, and he hugged me and told me everything was going to be all right. Whether or not he was telling the truth didn't matter; it was a nice thing to hear. Better still, Mr. Howland's hug gave me a substitute for the scary space-walk feelings about my mother being gone. Since then, we eat lunch together in his office most days and he checks in with me about how I'm feeling. While I'm admitting things, I'll tell you something else. When Mr. Howland held me and told me things were going to be okay, for a split second, I was glad my mother was sick.

If she hadn't gotten sick, I never would have cried and he never would have hugged me.

Mr. Howland's Birthday

MR. HOWLAND'S BIRTHDAY IS TODAY, April 3, and he says that what he wants for his birthday is a hickey. He knows that the girls in the class are all gaga over him, and the thought of giving him a hickey is driving me nuts. He doesn't say he wants the hickey from one of *us*, but he never mentions wanting it from his wife either. Patty is getting quite irritated because she doesn't like it when Mr. Howland jokes around and flirts. Patty and I can get pretty competitive about things. She wins in all areas academic; however, she is almost six feet tall, extremely thin, and in my opinion, she dresses like an old lady. She tends to wear long denim skirts and gauze hippie shirts that no one wears anymore, making her resemble an elongated version of Janis Joplin. Still, she cannot understand why Mr. Howland prefers me and not her; she has gotten an A+ on every single project, she sucks up to him, *and* she works harder than anyone else in the class. Unfortunately for her, those seemingly impressive facts are not what interest Mr. Howland. In fact, he seemed more interested in my cruddy mug than he did in Patty's fully functional tea bowl.

The hickey situation is making me insanely nervous. No doubt, Mr. Howland should not be joking with his students about having his neck sucked for his birthday, but on the other hand, it's exciting and fun to see Patty getting so pissed. All the girls are laughing, but no one except me is taking it seriously. We are supposed to be working on creating designs for our next project, my paper blank because I can't concentrate.

After Ceramics class, I spend the entire period in History imagining myself kissing Mr. Howland's neck. As I listen to Mr. Sikorsky drone on about the New Deal, I make a decision. It is time to test the waters. After classes end I have about twenty minutes before we have to leave for a tennis match. The next thing I know, I am standing in the hallway looking into Mr. Howland's empty classroom. The door to his small office in the back corner is open and the light is on. Out in the parking lot, a steady stream of faculty cars is bolting away from school as quickly as possible.

When Mr. Howland notices me, he doesn't say hello or what are you doing here or anything that indicates he is surprised to see me. His white shirt is untucked from his jeans, and he has clay stuck to his clothes. He glances around the room once. I am there and not there as he takes my hand and pulls me into his office. He kisses me and pushes his tongue down my throat and puts his hands into my back pockets and pulls my hips toward him. There are two of me at that moment, and both of us are important. One of me is inside my jeans and the other is invisibly patrolling the halls wondering who is going to come and catch us. I decide to stay with my body and feel his hands and his tongue for as long as possible. Anyone could walk in—our principal, Mr. Wright, or even Patty's mother coming by to senselessly flirt. Luckily, no one comes by, and we stay there kissing until I really have to go because I am going to be late for tennis.

That night I stay awake for half the night trying to convince myself that Mr. Howland actually kissed me. I go over every second of the kiss about a billion times, from the moment I walked into the room until I told him I had to go. I can barely sleep. My body is vibrating; each time I wake up (about every ten minutes), I feel like I am levitating and I have to grab the sheets to make sure I am not about to fly away. I'm happy thinking about the kiss, but at the same time I'm worried that Mr. Howland will change his mind and pretend it didn't happen. I flash back to a night last fall at Patty's house—Patty and I were upstairs getting ready to go out to a Halloween party. The Howlands were downstairs with Patty's mom. I was trying to say impressive things loud enough for Mr. Howland to hear while pretending to be focused on curling my hair into a sexy witch style. Then, as we were about to leave, Mr. Howland brought his guitar in from the car and sat down on the couch. He played and sang "Maggie May" by Rod Stewart, a song I love, and another song, a folk song about a woman living alone in a lighthouse. I watched Mr. Howland's wife as he played, and I thought that she had heard him too many times to appreciate how amazing he was. His blond, shaggy hair fell in his eyes as he strummed. I would never claim to like folk music, but Mr. Howland made me love it. Patty wanted to get to the party, but I wanted to stay. I wanted to skip that party and stay

there in my costume listening to Mr. Howland play that guitar for as long as I could.

My Job

FOR ALMOST A YEAR NOW, two or three nights a week and
sometimes on Saturday I've worked in a pharmacy in Farmington, a swanky little town a few miles from where I live. My
boss is a guy who thinks he looks exactly like Elvis Presley
did before he got all fat and beady-eyed and swollen-looking.
His name is Emory McDevitt. A funny thing about him is
that, despite his obvious obsession with the fact that he resembles Elvis, he calls Elvis "that Presley fellow." His voice
even sounds a tiny bit like Elvis's because he is from Ten-
nessee.

"Smiley," he says, "people think I look like that Presley
fellow."

"You mean Elvis," I say.

Emory calls me Smiley even though my real name is
Edna. As you can imagine, I don't mind being called Smiley,
as almost any name is better than Edna. Emory claims I am
smiling at all times, even when I am doing mundane tasks
like stocking shelves or counting pills. I never realized I was
constantly smiling until Emory pointed it out to me. Now,
when I catch Emory looking at me, I try to look serious.
Whether it is cold or hot outside, Emory sets the thermostat
inside the pharmacy at about forty-five degrees. He keeps the

temperature so frosty cold, I think, to prevent the black shoe polish he puts in his hair from running down his neck in watery streaks, which it does anyway, and staining the collars of his white or pink oxford shirts. Though I don't have any proof, I suspect that Emory is having an affair with at least two of the women who shop in the pharmacy. It would be difficult to say which women, because every attractive woman gets an equal amount of Emory's time and attention. The other night he spent an entire hour helping a gorgeous brunette in a tennis outfit pick out a birthday card for her husband.

About once a week, Emory gives me twenty bucks and sends me down to Cumberland Farms for cans of V8 to mix with the vodka that he keeps in the insulin refrigerator, and he never remembers to ask for the change. Emory drives a gigantic maroon Lincoln Continental that is dented and smashed in—he won't fix it because he believes his car has special lifesaving powers. My personal theory about why he has survived so many crashes is that, when he hits something, he's usually had a few Bloody Marys and his body is completely relaxed. Emory is good evidence that intoxicated people are survivors. It's the sober people who get killed.

Emory is obviously not a perfect person, but he is not a pervert. Many of the men his age I have spent time with have said something weird to me or even tried something perverted with me. At my last job, the two guys who ran the delicatessen were always asking me to come over and watch videos with them. I was only fifteen, but I knew what they meant. I even had a priest massage my neck at a church social and sort of kiss my shoulder. Not Emory. Emory has some sort of internal moral code, and even if I don't understand what it is, I believe it is similar to my own.

I steal stuff from the pharmacy, and I do feel bad about it, but as far as I can tell, Emory is not going to take inventory any time soon. Needing the things I take is not the issue, and Emory would most likely give me the stuff I steal if I bothered to ask. There is something about the butterflies I get in my stomach as I shove those two packs of Marlboro Lights in my tan Le Sportsac that is motivating me. It is a pretty addictive sensation. In addition to the packs of smokes, I take batteries for my radio from behind the counter, but I never take anything expensive. Besides, the expensive stuff in the pharmacy is not anything I'd ever want. Who would want a carved wooden statue of a druggist or a doctor? Maybe my father, though his collection of wooden creatures is made up primarily of Chinese people and small animals, so I don't even go into the gift section unless I am pretending to dust.

The biggest thief, however, is Mrs. McDevitt herself. About a week before Mr. Howland's kiss, when I was working the register by the front door, she walked in wearing a sequined dress and gold high-heeled shoes and headed down the antacid aisle. I could see the top of her curly red hair as she hurried to the pharmacy counter, where Emory, sporting the official white pharmacy coat that he almost never wears, was filling a prescription. Because of the light FM station that plays the same five songs on a continuous loop and the fact that they stepped into the office, I could not hear what they were saying. She was definitely shouting. After she came out, I heard the unmistakable *ding* of the pharmacy register and then seconds later watched Emory's wife make a beeline for the front door. It was not surprising when she didn't wave goodbye to me because she doesn't acknowledge my existence. I received a "come back here" buzz from Emory, and when I got to the pharmacy counter, Emory's pink shirt was turning black. Black droplets were running down his neck and collecting in a big dark stain on the edge of his collar.

"That son of a bitch," Emory hissed. "She's going to goddamned Atlantic City."

Standing next to me was Dale, the other clerk at the pharmacy, who is somewhat younger but seems much older than I am. Dale wears round wire-rimmed glasses and has hair so blond it looks white. He could almost be cute in a nerdy John Denver sort of way if he weren't so serious all the time. Dale is planning to go to Georgetown University when he graduates a year early from high school. Dale may know more about and is definitely more responsible about being a pharmacist than Emory.

"If you see that witch within one hundred yards of this store, I want you to call the goddamned police," Emory said.

He walked into his office, probably to make himself a vodka and V8.

"What happened?" I asked Dale, who had been stocking shelves in the pain relief section and had a better angle to watch the fight.

"She took a full bottle of ten-milligram Valiums and emptied the register," Dale said.

When Emory emerged from the back office about an hour later, he was in a much better mood. The light from the phone had been on the whole time, so I figured he was talking to either one of his girlfriends or Oliver, his wife's country-singer father, who seems to like Emory a lot better than he likes his own daughter. Emory was carrying a beach chair still wrapped in plastic that he'd found in the closet, and he told us to leave him alone because he was on vacation in the tropics. He unfolded the beach chair and set it up behind the counter. After removing the plastic covering, he placed his drink in the circular drink holder and sat down. He closed his eyes, stretched out his long legs, and kept sort of chuckling to himself. I began to ask him a question about a prescription, but he waved his hand.

"God damn it, Smiley, don't bother me," he said. "Can't you see I'm on goddamned vacation?"

"Da Ya Think I'm Sexy?" came on, and Emory jumped up, ran to the radio, and turned the volume so loud that the few customers still in the store put down whatever they were looking at and left. After I locked the front door, but before the official closing time of nine o'clock, the phone rang, and of course all three of us knew who it was because Mrs. McDevitt called up and made phony suicide threats at least once a week. She and Emory have an exciting relationship.

"Suicide Time," Emory yelled from his beach chair. "Don't you touch that damn phone, Dale."

Emory knew from past experience that it was almost impossible for Dale not to answer the phone, him being so conscientious and responsible. We knew Emory's wife was on the other end of that line. And we knew that Emory would not go home or return the call—he would go to the Foxy Hound Bar to get loaded and then, most likely, crash his car without getting injured. I left that night while the phone was ringing.

My School

MY SCHOOL IS AN INTERESTING PLACE despite the fact that most of the kids don't want to be here and have no desire to learn anything. The first thing you should know is that Bruce Springsteen, a.k.a. the Boss, practically comes from my town. I wasn't going to mention his name; I was simply going to describe his music and let you figure it out, but it would have been obvious anyway. As I said, he is the Boss, and everyone in this school except for Mr. Howland, the older teachers, and the black kids, who are more into soul and R & B, pretty much worships him. Mr. Howland, however, insists the Boss actually has little or no talent. He goes on and on about a singer from the 1960s, a guy who would have been much, much better than Springsteen, but he killed himself. I always think blah, blah, blah when Mr. Howland begins his rant, because it seems to me that he is more than a little bit jealous of Bruce Springsteen. Mr. Howland normally has outstanding taste in everything, but it can get rather tiring to hear him go on and on about how popular music has degenerated since the sixties. He thinks there hasn't been any good music since then and that most everything has gotten corrupt and meaningless. I'm not saying he is completely wrong, because people who were teenagers in the sixties did care about politics and the environment a lot more than kids my age do. Still, it gets annoying to have the flaws of your generation constantly thrown in your face.

A few of the teachers in my school are still acting and dressing like hippies, wearing bell-bottoms and army jackets and round John Lennon glasses even though it is 1980. Quite a few of them either were in Vietnam or protested against it. It can be confusing trying to sort through it, as you can imagine.

What Mr. Howland doesn't understand, not having grown up in this town, is that the Boss's music does reflect both the bad and the good about this place in an honest way. Of course, a lot of the songs are about sad kids trying to get the hell out of here any way they can—on motorcycles or in cars or even on the backs of other people's motorcycles. Truthfully, I wonder how bleak times and places like this one can exist, times and places where no one seems to care much about anything. The Boss's music captures the black hole feeling that comes from living in a town where most people are bitter and disappointed about how things turned out in their lives. Patty's mom is bitter for several reasons. Patty's dad had a heart attack about five years ago, and Patty and her mom had to move from a pretty nice town near Philadelphia to this place. Now, Patty's mom has to teach at a school where kids don't really want to learn. Mr. Howland is bitter about being married and not being a famous artist or critic.

Especially bitter and angry is my history teacher, Mr. Sikorsky, who marks me late most days because his class comes after Mr. Howland's and I always hang around Ceramics for as long as I can. Every day Mr. Sikorsky stands outside his room as the hall empties out, his fat stomach hanging over his maroon polyester pants. "You'll be late to your own wedding, Edna," he says as I run past him flashing my late pass. Mr. Howland has always been pretty liberal about giving passes, but since the kiss, I've been late every single day.

Mr. Sikorsky brags about wearing the same jacket for seventeen years of teaching. The class is supposed to be American History, and it would be nice if we learned about anything other than the Great Depression, but we don't. He once spent an entire period describing in gruesome detail how the economy in the 1920s festered until it finally burst. He said the stock market was like a boil filled with pus. As you can imagine, Mr. Sikorsky is firmly in the non-hippie camp. In fact, other than the Great Depression, the only thing he seems interested in is how, in a general sense, hippies and protesters destroyed America. A kid in my class told me that Mr. Sikorsky's son killed himself after he came home from Vietnam, but I'm not sure that it's true. The fact remains: I haven't learned one single important thing about history all year.

When you think it over, it is kind of strange how we never use our class time to examine the most important aspects of history. If I were a history teacher, I'd want to discuss why the black kids and the white kids in my school never talk to one another or sit together or go to any of the same parties. I might investigate why a rumor that Black Panthers were coming to our town several years back to protest got everyone so scared they canceled the Memorial Day parade. I'd try to figure out why the great leaders from the 1960s, like JFK and Bobby Kennedy and Martin Luther King and Malcolm X, got assassinated and why people are still so pissed off about Vietnam and why the first president I remember had to resign from office. I might even spend a few class periods trying to figure out how a guy as talented as Bruce Springsteen could even *come* from a place like this. Those seem like interesting topics—but all we get is the Great Depression.

Cancer

WHAT I THINK when I think about cancer is yikes. Most people who know that my mother is in the hospital treat me differently now. Though I haven't specifically told anyone about it except Patty and Mr. Howland, in a town like this, bad news travels fast. At school, if I fail a test, like I did in Latin a while back, I get sympathy instead of scorn. In fact, Ms. Clewell made a point of keeping me after class to talk with me. From the look on her face, I could tell she knew all about my mother.

"I'm not sure what happened," I told her.

She stood there looking at me, holding the paper with the big red "56%" written across the top in red pen.

"Daphne," she said, "you usually score somewhere in the nineties."

It's true. Latin is my best subject. And Ms. Clewell may be one of the best teachers I have had in this otherwise crummy school. We complained to her that the kids in French class got to pick French names, so she let us pick Latin names. She let me pick Daphne even though the name comes from a Greek myth; the story is one of my favorites because in it a young girl begs Zeus to turn her into a tree. You might think being completely immobilized doesn't sound like much fun; however, I have always felt I wouldn't mind being a tree. The kid who sits next to me is a senior named Craig. He is only about four and a half feet tall, and his translations are almost always wrong, but he picked the name Nero, another impressive selection.

"Are you sure you're all right?" Ms. Clewell asked.

Whenever I'm asked how I am, especially when I am not that hot, I almost pass out. I don't like it when people inquire into my well-being, especially not people who actually seem concerned, the way Ms. Clewell seems concerned. Everyone in the class likes her; the boys have crushes on her because she is younger than the average teacher and she has very straight auburn hair and doesn't try to seem as though she is cool, which many younger teachers do. It made me particularly sad to see I had written *veni, vidi, vici*, another favorite Latin saying of Ms. Clewell's, at the bottom of the paper. We were both clear I hadn't conquered anything on that particular test.

Deserved or not, the cancer sympathy goes beyond just Ms. Clewell. When the parking lot monitor caught me sneaking out to get sandwiches at lunch, he didn't give me detention. In a way, my mother's illness is another kind of pass. Although it has made certain aspects of my life easier, the fact remains she could actually die. And there is no one at home for me to talk with except my father, who isn't exactly Mr. Chatty. He has his own dark, paneled private study. Sometimes, when I am lonely, I peek at him from around the corner and see what he is doing. Usually he is sitting in his big easy chair with his eyes closed, the television set to sports or history, or else he is wearing half-glasses and looking over a legal file from his office. He never notices me standing there watching him. The biggest difference since my mother left is the quietness. My father and I don't have much to say to each other.

Mr. Howland's Wife

IT IS FRIDAY NIGHT, more than a week since the kiss, and we are at Patty's house. By "we" I mean me, Patty, Patty's mom, Mr. Howland, and even Mrs. Howland. Patty's mother is getting drunk on wine and making it impossible for me to talk to

Mr. Howland. She and Mrs. Howland are smoking Newport 100s, nasty mentholated cigarettes, while Mr. Howland smokes his Winston Reds. They are smoking and drinking and talking, mostly about teachers and kids at our school. Patty's mom brings a lasagna and salad out of the kitchen and puts one of the corniest albums ever recorded, *The Best of Bread*, on the record player. No one knows about Mr. Howland and me except me and Mr. Howland.

"Did you know that Sawyer was a great football player?" Mrs. Howland asks me.

"No," I answer, "I didn't."

"You should see the trophies," she continues. "He must have about twenty of them."

"I was a pretty good wide receiver," Mr. Howland says. "I was recruited to play in college, but I decided to study art instead. Went for the big bucks." We laugh, knowing that teachers make crappy money.

"You should come to the house sometime," Mrs. Howland says to me. "Sawyer could show you his trophies."

Mr. Howland's wife is staring at me like she too feels sorry for me. She probably imagines me as that confused teenage girl with a bad crush on her teacher. Mr. Howland is giving me looks, raising his eyebrows and grimacing, expressions acknowledging how weird a situation this is. Patty keeps trying to get me to leave, but I am stuffing lasagna into my mouth and feeling glued to my chair. I can't stop watching them. Bread is singing a stupid song called "If," a song about stupid people falling in love.

I imagine myself and Mr. Howland in his office, and for a moment, the whole scene in Patty's dining room goes into slow motion. Mr. and Mrs. Howland's words start to run together in my mind, and I have to close my eyes and hold my head because my body feels like it is coming apart while pieces of me float out of my chair. I dig my nails into my palms until the scene returns to normal speed. My body is wet with perspiration, but no one notices. I'm at the point of having to get up and run outside when my body reassembles itself. When I can open my eyes and focus, Patty's mom is pouring more wine. Mr. and Mrs. Howland are laughing and smoking. When they tip their heads back, I see that both of them, especially Mr. Howland, have silver or gold caps on their teeth. His otherwise straight and healthy-looking teeth are actually in poor shape. I can't find a single uncapped tooth in his entire mouth. Sitting next to his wife, Mr. Howland looks older than he does at school, possibly because she calls him Sawyer, a name almost as weird as mine, and not Mr. Howland. Mr. Howland's wife is very attractive in an older-woman way. Her hair is dark brown with a few gray wisps and cut straight across at the chin. She works as a paralegal, Mr. Howland told me, but she's going to law school at night. She does look tired. Suddenly I get an irresistible impulse to try to make them happy, to make all of them, even Mrs. Howland, feel young and lighthearted again. I start entertaining them, telling funny stories about Tyrone Love and other things from art class. At the same time, irrational as it seems, I want to ruin everything and tell Patty's mother and

Mrs. Howland that I don't need to see Mr. Howland's stupid football trophies—that I have something better than a football trophy.

Tennis Practice

SINCE THE KISS IN THE OFFICE, Mr. Howland and I are spending more time alone together. I don't even bother going to History or Gym most days, and other than Ms. Clewell, no one seems too interested in which classes I attend and which I don't. The only thing I still take seriously is tennis practice, because I am the number one player on the team. Last season, my mother used to come to my matches. I'm not sure why she didn't stand next to the court and watch like the other mothers; instead, she drove to a spot across the road and watched from inside her car. She must have been nervous I would start double-faulting or hitting balls over the fence if I knew she was there. But I always knew where she was anyway. About one-third of the way into my match, I would turn my head, and parked across the street would be her brown and tan paneled station wagon. She always left before the match was over. As quickly as she came, the next time I looked, she'd be gone.

Today as I am practicing my serve, I see Mr. Howland walking toward the courts. The tennis courts are near the soccer fields, and both places are completely out of his way, so I know he must be coming to see me. He is wearing his

Ray-Ban sunglasses and a light blue windbreaker and walking quickly, trying to make it look like he is in a big rush to get somewhere important, but I see him staring at the courts, trying to locate me. I attempt to hit a few really hard serves to impress him, but my nerves get the best of me and my serves sail to the baseline. So instead of trying to impress, I grab a full hopper and start firing balls at him. I'm about fifty yards away, and I can tell that this girl Sarah on the next court has no idea what to think about what I am doing, but I almost hit him once or twice and there are tennis balls bouncing around his legs.

"Hey," he yells, "cut it out!"

By then, both Sarah and the number three singles player have started hitting balls in his direction, and he finally has to put his hands over his head and jog back toward the main building. My teammates think it is hilarious. The coach, Mrs. Schwimmer, is nowhere around; everyone knows she's probably hiding out in the main office with her boyfriend, who is the vice principal. We spend the rest of practice trying to hit soccer players with tennis balls.

The Beach

BELIEVE IT OR NOT, Mr. Howland was somewhat mad about the tennis balls. However, all is forgiven and we are sitting in his office in the art room. The office is really about the size of a large closet. There are a few metal bookshelves, lots of oversize art books, an office chair, and a stool like the ones out in the classroom. I sit on the stool. It is dark because Mr. Howland stretched a piece of black cloth across a wood frame, which he uses as a shade for the window that looks out to the faculty parking lot. One of Mr. Howland's secret plans is to order a bunch of art books and expensive supplies and then quit, take the expensive stuff with him, and pursue his career as an artist. I think it is a good idea, because as my father says, everyone needs to plan for the future.

Sitting in his office behind the black screen, I am happy. I love the fact that Mr. Howland is so creative and talented. Examining the titles of these beautiful books on art and artists, I firmly believe one day Mr. Howland will be either a famous artist with books written about him or a writer himself with books displayed on other teachers' shelves.

On Saturday afternoon, we had what I would call our first official date. We met in the parking lot of the Presbyterian church on West Street and then drove to the beach in his car. On the way we stopped for a sub. After we argued for a while about where to park, he grabbed a blanket and we headed down to the most deserted section. It was a warm day for April, but not so warm that I wasn't surprised to see a few men with their foil reflectors and their nut-snuggler bathing suits trying to catch some rays. We went so far down the beach that there was no one else within a hundred yards of us. The first thing we did was eat the sub, which was delicious, especially when alternating bites with potato chips and sips of soda. There was a nice, cool breeze coming off of the slightly choppy ocean, and the food tasted better than any food I've ever eaten.

"What a day," Mr. Howland said.

Mr. Howland's skin is rather fair, the kind of skin that probably freckles and burns rather than tans. He took off his shirt and lay down on the blanket, revealing his perfectly smooth chest. I pushed my finger into his belly button, and he squirmed before grabbing my wrist.

"What's the news on your mom?" he asked.

"I think she needs radiation," I told him, trying not to reveal how little I know about her actual condition.

"That's a bummer," he said.

"It's quiet in my house with my father gone all the time."

Mr. Howland squeezed my hand and then pulled me from my sitting position so that I was lying across his chest. He lifted my body on top of his and kissed my neck. There was something jabbing into my side from inside the pocket of his jeans. I didn't want to move because he was rubbing my back very softly.

"There's a sea creature in your pants," I finally said.

"Indeed there is," he replied. "An electric eel."

I've had two moderately serious boyfriends in my life, Jack Carson in eighth grade and Jeff Riddle last year, but we were quite innocent about the whole sexual thing. We mainly went to movies and didn't progress beyond making out. They were both pretty shy. I did go on a double date with Barbie last year over to the house of a high-profile senior named Mark Howell. After making us listen to him play the drums along with "Carry on Wayward Son" by Kansas about three times, Mark turned off the lights, and the other kid, a basketball player named Jimmy Keys, jumped on me and practically raped me with his clothes on. It was like being molested by a dog who won't stop grinding on your leg even when you hit it repeatedly with a magazine or a newspaper. Since then, I haven't really dated anyone. But I think I am finally ready for the next step.

I rolled off Mr. Howland and lay down next to him. I liked the feel of his soft skin, especially the skin on his sides. He turned toward me and put his arm across my stomach. Even with the presence of the eel, he didn't try to make me do anything. With his hand on my stomach, his fingers stretched from one side of my waist to the other. He measured my stomach with his outstretched hand, and we laughed at the smallness of me.

Now Mr. Howland looks out the door to make sure the classroom is empty before he kisses me, but I ruin the mood by bringing up the unmentionable.

"What about your wife?" I ask.

"Don't worry about that," he says.

"Who do you love best?" I ask him.

"I love you," he tells me. "I've loved you longer than you know."

I don't tell him, but I've loved him since Foodtown.

Waiting Around

BEING WITH MR. HOWLAND requires patience. When he tells me to meet him, he is invariably late and I end up waiting. It doesn't bother me because I've always been good at waiting. I like having a reason to do nothing but stare into space. When I was a little girl, it seemed like I was constantly waiting around for my father. Back when we still lived in town, before my father built our new house and moved us to the farm where we live now, my father used to take me and Barbie to our farm to ride the horses I don't ride anymore. If Barbie didn't come along, my father might stop on the way at boring places like auctions where broken or not broken pieces of farm equipment were being sold in big, dusty parking lots. My father loved inspecting the machinery, hay balers and tractors and machines without names with forked metal teeth for tearing through fields. While he walked around, he would forget about me. My father never looked as interested in anything as he did in those tractors and machines. He could spend hours wandering, pausing now and again to examine a machine more closely. He must have wished that he wasn't a lawyer when he stood there in those open lots. He probably wished he was a farmer who could ride around cutting hay all day long. In fall and winter, my father wore a red hunting coat that smelled of burning leaves and a red hat with wool-lined earflaps tied up with a leather string. He is tall and slim. His only flaw is that he walks with a slight limp that he got from being injured in the war.

There were Sundays when minutes passed like hours as I sat in our car feeling sick to my stomach before he would come back. While my father was walking around talking to real farmers, he treated those tractors and other machines as the only things that mattered in the entire world; he was not worrying about me—where I was or what I was doing or how nauseated my chronic car sickness might have left me. He walked and talked until he decided he had seen enough. And then, finally, at the moment I was ready to bolt from the car and grab his shirt, he turned and walked slowly back, away from the farming implements, and took me to the general store, where a very scary old man with bumps covering his head gave me a grape soda from an old refrigerator.

If he was feeling especially nice, my father let me shift gears on the way home. I moved over toward his seat and put my hand on the shifter. When it was time, he yelled "Now!" and I would push the stick into third or fourth gear. The best place to shift was at a stop sign at the top of a hill near a red stone church and a small graveyard. Starting from the stop sign, I would do the whole sequence of gears—first through fourth. On top of that hill was a good place to be because you had a view that stretched for miles. It may have been one of the highest spots in New Jersey. Like most great moments, however, it was short-lived. By the time you appreciated how high you were and how exciting it was, the car was in fourth gear and the magic was over.

I hardly see my father anymore. We pass in the hallway at night, but he is gone before I even get up in the morning.

And then he has left work and gone to New York to see my mother in the hospital when I get home from school. If we do happen to be in the house at the same time, I tend to avoid him because he always asks me to go to the city with him to see my mother. It has been a long time since I went to a farm auction, and I guess that should make me happy because they really were dead boring. I'll tell you this: I wouldn't mind it one bit if he took me to that general store for a grape soda. I'd go with him even if it meant I had to look at that bumpy-headed old guy one more time.

Distance

MY FATHER TAUGHT ME EVERYTHING about distance. On Thursday nights during the summer from the deck of our beach house, I would watch the fireworks with him. We sat all wrapped up in a blanket, and he explained why the bang came so long after the flash—five seconds for every mile. My father knew this from having fired artillery shells during World War II. Distance was everything. Maybe he didn't remember, or maybe it was so important it needed repeating, but he told me the same thing every time. He held me there and told me how many seconds and how many miles. He could always calculate how far away things were. It went like this: fireworks—one Mississippi two Mississippi three Mississippi four Mississippi five Mississippi BANG! During the school year, our house is rented. Otherwise, Mr. Howland

and I would go there and I could show him the exact spot over the ocean where the fireworks would explode.

Tonight, when I go downstairs to get a drink of water, my father is asleep. I go to the closet in the hallway and dig through my mother's raincoat and fake fur and my old windbreakers and team jackets until I find that red hunting coat. There is a grease stain on the collar and the sleeves are dirty, but I bury my face in that coat until I think I can smell the burning leaves.

My Brother

I don't usually mention it because the whole thing is somewhat complicated, but for some reason I tell Mr. Howland about my older brother, who died when I was very small. We are sitting in his car, which makes sense because most of our alone time is spent either in the car or hiding out in his office. We are parked in the corner of the giant lot in front of Britt's department store. Mr. Howland is talking to me about his brother, whose name is Tom. He lives in Virginia. It's funny to me that his name is Tom.

"Wait," I say. "Your brother's name is Tom and your name is Sawyer?"

He gets mad so I stop laughing and change the subject.

"I used to have a brother," I say.

"What do you mean you used to have a brother?" he says.

"His name was Tommy. He died a long time ago."

"What did he die of?" he asks.

"I don't know," I say. "He had some disease called autism, and the strangest part is that he never learned to talk. Other than that, my parents haven't really told me much about him."

"I'm sorry," Mr. Howland says.

And then he tries to console me the way people console each other. He hugs me, expecting me to be upset, the way people expect me to be upset about my mother, but I am not upset. I sit there in his arms feeling frozen while he tells me how sorry he is and how terrible it is to lose someone.

What I don't mention to him, what I've never told anyone, is that Barbie asked me once if my brother was murdered by a psychiatrist. We were only about ten or eleven years old, but I never forgot. She made it sound as though she knew something I didn't. I was sleeping over at her house and she asked me about my brother right in the middle of a game of Barbie dolls. She acted like she figured I would know the answer, but the truth is no one ever told me how he died. The extent of what I know is that he was six years old, he couldn't talk, and he was living with a psychiatrist. I have no idea how I answered her or if I even answered her at all. A few days later, a day when I was in one of my most worried and least talkative moods, I asked my mother if I could get autism and she said no. She told me it was something you were born with. The fact that I knew how to speak at the time convinced me that she was right, that I must be normal.

To be honest, it would be good to know what happened

to my brother. Maybe the psychiatrist he was living with got so mad at him for not talking that she murdered him. I know from experience that people don't like it when you clam up. Or maybe he died of something else. It is hard to believe someone murdered him, but once a seed gets planted in your mind, it's difficult to root it out.

"Do you ever talk to your parents about him?" Mr. Howland asks.

"Not really," I tell him. "I did read an article about autism in *Reader's Digest* one time. They used to say it was the parents' fault."

"That's all crap, right?" Mr. Howland asks.

"Yeah, but they still have no idea what happens."

"Doctors," Mr. Howland says, shaking his head. "Never trust doctors or lawyers."

He seems to have forgotten that my father is a lawyer and his wife is studying to become one. Mr. Howland leaves me in the car while he goes to get me a soda. I'm tempted to open the glove compartment and seek evidence of his wife, but I decide that it will only make me feel lousy if I do.

Me and a Psychiatrist

I AM GOING TO SEE A PSYCHIATRIST on Wednesday. My mother is actually forcing me to go from the hospital because she must think she isn't going to come home. She was already talking about getting me counseling before she got sick because of my sinking grades and refusal to talk about anything with her, but the idea of seeing an actual doctor feels a bit extreme to me. My father seems irritated at the idea, but I can imagine why he might not be too hot on psychiatrists. His response was, "I wish I could afford to be psychotic." He can't afford to have any mental issues because he has to work almost all of the time. The last time he took a day off was for Expo '67, when I was around four years old. But he did buy me a very nice little car, a green Triumph TR7. I can't stress enough how cool this car is. Most of my friends drive their mothers' station wagons or beat-up El Caminos. Believe me, if my mother was home, I never would have gotten a car this nice. The best part about the whole thing is that the psychiatrist's office is pretty far away and I'll get to drive my new Triumph.

Mr. Howland doesn't think the psychiatrist is the greatest idea, and I can't say I blame him. He's probably afraid I am going to spill my guts about him kissing me and whatnot in his office. But he can rest assured. I definitely will not spill my guts. I am not an idiot. Being with Mr. Howland, no matter where we are, is my favorite place to be, besides driving my new car. Why would I risk blowing the only outstanding things in my life right now? The truth is that I don't know what the hell I'll say to that stupid psychiatrist. Because I am not sad that my mother is gone. I'm really not.

The Psychiatrist

I AM THE ONLY PERSON in the waiting room. I am wearing my most colorfully patched jeans and my father's white shirt with a frayed collar. My mother would flip out if she saw me. She believes in getting dressed up when you go to the doctor and when you fly on a plane, among other places. I never could make sense of it, but now that she isn't around to monitor me, I can wear whatever I want. I felt awesome driving here in my new Triumph with the roof down in my too-casual-for-the-doctor outfit, even though I forgot my cassettes and had to listen to stupid songs on the radio for the entire ride. The only things missing were some cool sunglasses and a cigarette. And of course, it would have been better if I were going somewhere other than a psychiatrist's office.

I have to sit there alone before the doctor comes out to get me. There are a few framed prints on the wall in the waiting room. My favorite is a watercolor of some colorful fish swimming in a bowl. It is one of those prints you see in every doctor's office and reception area, but I like it anyway.

When he opens the door, Dr. Chester isn't wearing a white coat and carrying a pinwheel with which to hypnotize me; he is wearing a tan poplin suit and he is going bald and he doesn't seem to care one bit what I am wearing, which just proves me right about it not mattering. He escorts me into the office, where he sits behind a large oak desk and I sit across from him in a pretty comfortable chair, but not as comfortable as the big leather bend-back chair he gets to sit in, of course. Over by the plaques on the wall is a couch, which looks more like what a psychiatrist might ask you to lie down on while you do free association, but he doesn't seem to want me to move. He sits there like a stump for a while not talking, slowly nodding his head. One of the plaques says that he graduated from Harvard Medical School, and I don't know whether or not I should be impressed. Seems like he might be too much psychiatrist for what I need.

"I don't have any major problems," I tell him. "I'm only here because my mother said I had to come."

"Is that why you are here?" he asks.

"Yeah," I say, "I just told you that. She has cancer, so I couldn't really say no, could I?"

He nods some more, and I think maybe I should use this chance to talk about how I spent most of my childhood afraid of contracting or developing a fatal disease. My parents banned me from watching *Medical Center* and reruns of *Dr. Kildare* back in elementary school because every week I had a brand-new set of symptoms. My mother got so tired of listening to me complain about things like ringing in my ears, the inability to swallow, blinding headaches, brain tumors, and so forth that she finally decided I couldn't watch any more doctor shows. I could also report to this doctor that I hesitate before taking vitamins or aspirin for fear of being accidentally poisoned. I could also kill time by making stuff up the way I did when I had to go to confession, but I don't want him to wrap me up in a straitjacket or anything. I decide to feign normalcy.

"How is your mother?" he asks.

"Well," I say, "I think she is all right. My father goes and sees her every night, but I haven't been able to go because I'm busy with school and tennis and lots of other things."

He keeps nodding. I figure he is about to get angry or at least realize that I have given a completely lousy excuse for not even once visiting my mother, who could die in the hospital, but he just sits there, his bald head bobbing up and down.

"Are you worried about your mother?" he asks.

I wonder if I should be worried about the fact that I don't seem to have feelings. I think he is waiting for me to start talking, to confide in him about kissing Mr. Howland, and about eating that sub on the beach, and about how my mother getting cancer has so many unexpected benefits, but instead I sit there slumped down in my sort of comfortable chair chewing on my nails.

"Of course I'm worried," I say.

"Do you think it might help if you saw her?"

"I don't know," I reply. "It's possible, but I don't think so."

The thought of going down Niagara Falls in a barrel is less scary than the thought of visiting my mother in the hospital.

"It might help," he says.

"It might," I admit.

But my stomach is once again hardening up and sending a crystal clear message to my brain not to visit her. I listen to the message.

"I was fighting with her, you know," I say. "Right before she left."

"What about?" he asks.

"The usual stuff," I tell him. "Parties and whatnot."

"I'm sure she won't hold it against you," he says. "She's probably forgotten about the fight by now."

I don't tell him how she said our fight was *postponed*, not canceled. For a guy with so many impressive degrees on the wall, Dr. Chester doesn't seem to get that there are some things you just don't talk about—topics that can create fissures and tidal waves that swallow everything around them. There are words you should not say, no matter how much you might want to say them. It puzzles me that he could be a high-powered shrink and not know something that is so obvious to someone as young as I am.

He finally asks me a question or two about my life and I give some generic answers and I'm getting convinced this psychiatric thing is a big fat waste of time and money. I'm exhausted from watching what I say and pretending to be fine and then finally it is time to leave. I go out a different door from the one I came in through, one that doesn't require me to go through the waiting room, where I could potentially encounter the next patient. It's like a secret exit. I see my beautiful Triumph and can't wait to drive away.

Home

DURING THE WEEK, Dad leaves me to get dinner by myself. Mostly I eat unhealthy crap like Whoppers or Big Macs with fries and a vanilla shake. But it does give me a chance to sit on the front steps and smoke the cigarettes I steal from the pharmacy. I finally learned to blow perfectly O-shaped smoke rings, but I can't blow smoke in two thin streams from my nostrils the way Mr. Howland's wife can. For some reason, smoke will only come out of my left nostril, probably, I imagine, a symptom of something horrible like a nostril tumor or something.

Though she quit a long time ago, my mother used to smoke. After she had washed the dinner dishes and straightened up the kitchen, she liked to sit in her chair in the living room and read a book and smoke. She loves reading. And I have to say that she reads interesting and well-written books, not the kinds of books that other mothers read—crappy supermarket books and romance novels. My mother reads books on religion and anthropology. When I was younger, eight or nine, I remember her reading a book called *The Naked Ape*, which I thought was a dirty book because there were naked people on the cover, but I found out later that it isn't. She told me she likes to read books about families. The fact that she spent most of her free time reading sometimes made me wonder if she liked reading about other families more than she liked having one, but I didn't ask that. It could be she and my father found out there are some pretty big

negatives about the whole family thing. I did ask her, however, what happens to people when they die. She was smoking when I asked her, and she paused to ponder the question
for a while before she said, "I don't know. I think it's probably something like before you were born."

That thought wasn't exactly comforting, because I was
still hoping for angels with giant white wings and God himself and trumpets and maybe even an entire city of clouds
and glitter, but lately I think her idea might not be so bad after all.

Some nights while she read, I'd sit on the floor and play
Monopoly with my invisible half-human, half-chipmunk
friend, Sucan. My mother is not a big fan of board games; in
fact, she especially hates Monopoly, so she was happy to let
me pretend that Sucan existed. Other times, my mother let
me sit on her lap, even though I was probably too big to be
doing so. What I liked best was to push myself against her
soft body, hiding my face in the space between her arm and
her breast while she read to herself.

Heaven

"DO YOU BELIEVE IN HEAVEN?" I ask Dr. Chester.

"Why do you ask?" he says, once again answering a question with a question, a tactic I've noticed he employs quite
regularly.

"I'm just wondering," I say.

"Are you worried about your mother?" he asks.

"I'm pretty sure she doesn't believe in Heaven," I tell him.

I did go to Sunday school for a few years, but I can hardly remember anyone saying anything about Heaven other than that all children who die go to Heaven because Jesus likes little kids better than older people.

"Would you want to talk to your mother about religion?" he asks.

"My mother was my Sunday school teacher when I was in second grade," I explain. "But we didn't really go into God or Jesus very much. We made a biblical village out of soap once."

"Did you enjoy Sunday school?" he wants to know.

"Building the soap village was fun," I tell him. "And I liked this kid named Richie, who used to draw pictures of Jesus riding a motorcycle."

"Would you ever think about going back to church?" he asks.

"I don't think so," I respond. "I'm really not the church type. My mother isn't the church type either, but my father is. Maybe he's got the whole family covered," I say.

Dr. Chester spends the rest of my time trying to get me to talk about my parents and my feelings about them, but to be honest, this is not a subject I actually gravitate toward at the moment.

A Sculpting of Me

IT'S THURSDAY AFTERNOON, the day after therapy, and we are sitting in Mr. Howland's office before tennis practice. No one is in the building except for us and maybe a few janitors. Mr. Howland tells me he has a surprise. He is full of surprises lately. Today's surprise is artistic. He takes a sculpture out from behind some books.

"Is that me?" I ask.

"Yes, it is," he says.

"How could anybody tell?"

It is a valid question. The sculpture has no face; it is of my torso from my breasts to my hip bones. No arms, legs, or head. It is made from clay, and I can see the gentleness with which he has sculpted me. He even got my belly button exactly right. The more I look, the more I recognize my body. He must have studied my stomach pretty carefully that day at the beach.

"Why didn't you include my face?" I ask.

"Because I love your stomach," he says. "You have a perfect stomach."

I've never really given much thought to my stomach. When I think about myself, I tend to focus on my face and my hands; my hands because the nails and cuticles are torn up from being chewed and bitten. I try to hide them as much as possible. Sometimes I find I've been tearing away at them for an hour and don't even remember, like I've been in some kind of trance.

Mr. Howland has a graduate degree in art history. He published his thesis in an art journal, and he loves to study paintings. He thinks of himself as a sculptor, but the work I've seen of his is all pretty modern and experimental. He has a piece on a shelf in the back of the room that resembles a giant clamshell, but I'm afraid to ask him if that is exactly what it is supposed to be. He brought it in as an example when our assignment was to make protection for ourselves, sort of like a shell an animal might have for protection. I made a helmet and some wristbands, which earned me a C+. Mr. Howland loves to go on about balance and proportion, and positive and negative space. The only person in the class who seems to have any idea what he is talking about is Patty.

After we admire my body, Mr. Howland tells me about the place that he has found for us to go, a secret place out in the woods. I know what he is thinking. He needs a place he can take me, a secluded place where there is no chance that anyone like a Latin teacher or a principal or even sunbathers can come and surprise us. I want to go. I want to go wherever he wants to take me. He is sick of hiding, he says, and he wants to be alone with me. The plan is, on the day of our trip to the secret spot, I will tell the tennis coach, Mrs. Schwimmer, I have to go to New York to see my mother in the hospital, which is the perfect excuse because it seems impossible that anyone could doubt me or check up on me. So, I will be clear for the entire afternoon.

Don't think that I don't have some remorse about it—using my mother for an excuse when I haven't been to see her in the hospital since the day we dropped her off, a day I remember quite well because I had to stay home from school and ride all the way to New York in the backseat of my father's car, which even under ordinary circumstances makes me queasy. My mother rode in the front, her eyes closed and her head leaning on the headrest. She didn't talk except to answer my questions. I was feeling too sick to my stomach to go inside, I told them, so my father checked her in by himself while I waited in the parked car for about an hour. My mother kissed me when she got out, but I could tell that she wasn't really thinking much about me. When my father finally came back, he said they'd be taking her in for tests.

He hasn't *insisted* I visit her since then, but I know he's upset with me for not going. The other night, after we ate the pizza he brought home, he looked at me like he was going to grab me and shove me into the trunk of his car and force me to go with him, but he is too stubborn to do something like that. My father is very quiet and forceful in his own way, but we are pretty well matched when it comes to being stubborn. I won't go to New York, and as my mother would say, that is all there is to it. But I am happy to be going with Mr. Howland to the secret spot, wherever it is.

Peter Robin

IT IS DIFFICULT TO REMEMBER when my father started or stopped telling me the stories about Peter Robin. It was obviously before we stopped talking to each other. Because there was a time when he used to come into my room at night and sit on my bed and make up adventures about a bird named Peter Robin, who was always getting himself into trouble. Peter Robin was the kind of bird who couldn't help but go places and do things that his mother specifically told him not to. He almost got killed about a million times. Once, he caught his foot on the horns of a bull that was charging a farmer. I remember the story well because it was clear from the description that my father was thinking of himself when he described the farmer. At the last possible second, the farmer stepped out of the way and grabbed Peter Robin off the horns of the bull, saving his life once again.

The best part came right before the ending. My father put his hand in front of my face and made all his fingers flutter like the wings of a bird. He said, "Close your little eyes," and made his fingers fly down over my eyelids so that I would have to close them. When I think about it now, it is hard to imagine my father ever sitting on the end of my bed pretending to be a bird. I can't even remember the last time he came up to my room.

Another Visit to the Shrink

"HAVE YOU EVER HEARD OF AUTISM?" I ask. I ask casually because I'm not sure if I want to talk about this. The word "autism" has always bothered me because it somehow got associated with the word "mannequin" in my mind, and mannequins scare me.

"Yes," says Dr. Chester. "Why?"

"My brother died of it," I say.

"I don't think you die from autism," he says. He looks at me. "Did someone tell you that your brother died from autism?"

"I know he had it and he died," I tell him. "He never learned to talk."

"Why didn't you tell me about your brother before?"

"Because I'm telling you now."

I am instantly regretting I have brought this up because I can see that Dr. Chester thinks this is a very big deal. He usually slumps down in his chair, but now he's sitting up and he's paying close attention, like he thinks that my brother could provide one of the secret keys to understanding me.

"Your brother died?" he asks.

"Yes," I say.

"And how old was he?"

"I think he was six."

"Do you remember him?"

"I was only one when he died," I say. "How could I remember him?"

But that isn't really the truth. I've always had this weird memory of sitting on the sand in front of our beach house watching my brother and my father collecting shells. My brother has blond hair, and he is wearing a red-and-white-striped bathing suit. He is looking carefully around the sand for interesting objects. My father is walking near him holding a yellow plastic bucket. That is the memory. It might even be a dream I had.

"Did you ever ask your mother and father how he died?"

"No," I say. "They never bring it up, so I don't want to start a conversation that might hurt their feelings."

"You mean your parents' feelings?"

"I don't want to dredge up bad memories."

"How did you find out about him?"

"My mother told me," I say, words suddenly pouring out. "My mother told me he died while he was living with a psychiatrist from Johns Hopkins University. He was living with her in Maine for the summer. She was trying to help him get better. My mother said that I wasn't autistic and that I never would be. She probably figured I'd start worrying *I* was autistic, which I naturally did anyway, the way I thought I had every other disease in the world. It was weird because she told me this stuff while we were standing in her bathroom in our old house. I wasn't in that bathroom very often. She was holding something in her hand, maybe a comb or lipstick, and we were looking in the mirror, talking to our mirror images. I remember thinking about the pink tiles on the walls and the way the black ones were mixed in sort of randomly. I remember that because I wanted there to be a pattern in the tiles."

I stop and take a breath.

"Do you know anything else about his death?" Dr. Chester asks.

"Well," I say, "I do know one thing." As I talk I realize Dr. Chester will be the first person I've told something that I never wanted to tell anyone. I didn't even tell this part to Mr. Howland. "When I was about eleven years old, my friend Barbie asked me if he was murdered by a doctor."

"You never found out if this was true?" Dr. Chester asks, like he can't quite believe that I wouldn't have found out. But how can I find out things if no one ever talks about them?

"I guess I could have found out," I say. "I'm not sure why I never did."

I am starting to hate Dr. Chester for prying into my life.

"Is it common for psychiatrists to kill autistic people?" I ask.

"No," he says, "it isn't."

My attempt to get him angry falls flat.

"You could ask your father," he says.

"We don't talk too much," I remind him.

It's weird because I have a strange sense that Dr. Chester already knows what happened to my brother and he's not telling me. I often get the feeling that people know something I don't know, as though I missed the meeting where they gave out the most vital information about everything, information about when and how to have sex and how my brother died and whether or not my mother is going to come home soon from the hospital. It would be exactly like me to miss that kind of meeting.

I remain silent and wonder if I said anything that might

make Dr. Chester think I'm crazy. I am regretting even bringing up my brother and autism more than I can say.

"How is school?" Dr. Chester asks.

"All right," I answer, relieved he sensed my need for a change of subject. "Except I'm not doing so well in Latin, which is strange because Latin is my best subject. It's really the only subject besides Ceramics I'm doing well in at the moment."

"Really," he says.

"I failed a pretty big test a while back, but she let me take it over again," I say.

"The teacher?" he asks.

"Her name is Ms. Clewell, and she is actually a very good teacher. I think she feels sorry for me because of my mother."

"Maybe she is someone you could talk to?" he asks hopefully, recognizing it probably isn't going to be my father.

"Maybe," I answer.

Talking with Ms. Clewell would be perfectly fine with me except for the fact that I believe she may have some sort of radar out on me and Mr. Howland. A few times while he and I have been eating lunch, she has popped her head in to say hi or ask him a random question about an upcoming meeting. She even came in once and wandered around, pretending to admire the stupid art projects. Mr. Howland thinks she drops by because she is crazy about him, but I'm not so sure. I question the motives behind those pop-ins.

"By the way," I begin, "what causes someone to be autistic?"

"I'm sorry to say that there is no one theory that adequately explains the cause."

"Is it the mother's fault?" I ask.

"Some doctors used to try to explain it as an attachment disorder, but no one studying the disease holds that view. Blaming parents adds insult to injury for people dealing with a heartbreaking problem."

"I read a magazine article about that," I tell him.

"Are you interested in reading more about autism?"

"No," I tell him. "I think I know enough."

Dr. Chester asks several more questions about how things are going, but I'm already thinking about Mr. Howland and where he is going to take me when he finally takes me to the secret spot. I don't mention this to Dr. Chester, but the truth is that I am beginning to think about Mr. Howland more than ever. Lately, before I go to sleep, I go over everything we said to each other that day, even the boring kinds of exchanges that happen during class or over lunch. Some nights, the only way I can get to sleep is by remembering I will see him the next day. I squeeze my pillow and experience waves of love like tidal waves so strong I think I might roll out of bed. I would like to ask Dr. Chester whether these are normal responses to being in love. Is love supposed to feel like a sickness?

Driving home from Dr. Chester's office, I can't get the pink-and-black bathroom out of my head. While I was talking about my brother, I remembered going into that bathroom to hide when I was mad. I'd sit on the toilet, even if I didn't need to, and ask myself over and over again, Who do you love most: your mother, your father, or God? I knew the right answer was God, but I also knew that if I said God, I wouldn't be telling the truth. The problem was there was no answer that was definitely right or true. It was the kind of question I wished I didn't need to ask myself.

The Dracula Principle

MR. HOWLAND KNOWS ALL ABOUT DRACULA. He believes we can learn everything we need to know from Dracula. According to Mr. Howland, Count Dracula's success came from his power to move about freely. Dracula had this power because no one really wanted to believe that a vampire could exist. Mr. Howland says that most people don't want to acknowledge possibilities that they don't understand. So, we need to operate under what Mr. Howland calls "the Dracula Principle." If people don't believe something is possible, then they won't see it even when it is right in front of their eyes.

Mr. Howland explains the Dracula Principle to me while we sit at one of the dirty tables in his classroom waiting for his hamburger to finish cooking. The meat sizzles and spits on the hot plate. Mr. Howland read somewhere that hamburgers eaten at the same time as tomato wedges cause a chemical reaction that will make him lose weight. Sadly, I have a ham sandwich I made myself, just two slices of ham on white bread. Before she went away, my mother used to make me lunch every morning. She made interesting sandwiches like cream cheese with olives and roast beef with pickles. Mr. Howland cuts the tomato into pale pink wedges and places them around the edge of a paper plate. The pink juices from the meat and the tomato stream in rivulets, forming red, greasy puddles that are finally absorbed into the white paper. His whole plate is turning wet from the blood.

"Guess what?" Mr. Howland says.

"What?" I say.

"Tomorrow is the day."

"What day?" I ask.

"The day I show you a surprise."

"A good surprise?" I ask.

"What other kinds of surprises are there?" he asks.

"Bad ones," I say.

"This is a good one," he says.

He tells me I should meet him at the church after practice. He lifts the hamburger to his mouth, and as he opens wide, I see the gold caps on the backs of his teeth. He looks pretty happy. I'm wondering where this secret spot could be. There are housing developments everywhere you go around here. The only wooded places are near my parents' house, and I don't believe I want to be anywhere near there. Mr. Howland looks calm, and I am getting excited already, when I begin to wonder a bit about whether or not this is a great idea. Mr. Howland's increasingly complicated plans only work if the

Dracula Principle operates the way he says it does. His plate is now completely saturated with red juice, which is causing the paper to disintegrate—the chemical reaction is certainly working on the paper. A stream of juice is running off the edge of the paper plate and pooling up on the table, but Mr. Howland doesn't notice.

Today no one has stopped by to say hello—no Patty's mother coming by to be sexy, no random pop-in from my Latin teacher, and no girls who simply have crushes on Mr. Howland. Aside from Ms. Clewell, I wonder if people think it is odd that I'm always in here eating lunch with Mr. Howland. He is putting the last tomato wedge into his mouth, completing the reaction that will cause him to become thin. Clay from someone's project coats the table. The sculpture of my body is on the shelf next to Mr. Howland's office door, a risky idea if you ask me, but, following his principle, Mr. Howland thinks people are too stupid to notice.

That night, lying in bed, I go over our conversation about the secret spot. The intensity of the excitement I feel is making my knees ache. My mind is a broken record. "This is really going to happen," I say over and over to myself. Each time I say it, my stomach seizes up and I experience that feeling again of rolling in giant waves. Finally, I get up and put on *Moondance*, thinking it might help me to calm down. By the time the record gets to "Into the Mystic," I'm ready to sleep.

The Secret Spot

To GET TO MR. HOWLAND'S SECRET SPOT, we have to drive about three miles out of town. We are getting sort of out in the direction of my parents' house, and I start to feel on edge, but then we make a left turn on a road that I've never seen before. It is called Silo Road, and the name gives me the creeps because I picture myself getting trapped inside a silo like Rapunzel, alone for the rest of my life with no one to save me. There aren't many houses on Silo Road; the houses I see have falling-down porches made from cinder blocks. I start to think I recognize the trees and the curves in the road. I believe we are somewhere near a pond I used to skate on called Goose Pond. Because this is New Jersey, the pond only froze hard enough to skate on once or twice a winter, and those times were big deals for everyone. It's funny. I've been to Goose Pond many times, but I never knew exactly where it was. I never notice anything. I never know how I got anywhere, and if someone left me in the woods, I'd probably die before I found my way out. One thing I remember about skating was that, in order to get to the pond, you had to walk in your ice skates down a hill lined with wood chips, and it wasn't easy.

"This is near Goose Pond," I announce to Mr. Howland.

"What is Goose Pond?" he asks.

Mr. Howland grew up in Richmond, Virginia, nowhere near here. He has never climbed that wood chip hill, trying to dig his blades into the loosely packed chips to get a foothold but always being on the verge of breaking an ankle and sliding down toward the frozen pond. Mr. Howland doesn't remember "the whip," a line of about twenty boys who skated together on the dark side waiting for a girl to skate over so they could knock her down. This is not familiar to Mr. Howland, and it isn't familiar to me anymore because we've gone past the road that would have taken us to the pond. We've gone farther than I have ever been in this direction.

We turn onto a dirt road that leads through branches and tall grass and runs into a clearing. It looks almost like someone took a scythe and prepared this place for us to find it. This is the secret spot, and I try not to think about Mr. Howland driving around out here by himself searching for this location. And this car-size clearing waiting for people like us to find it. Down a short path from the clearing is a small barn, almost like a place you'd keep tack. It looks completely abandoned. There is nothing but bare walls and a wood floor.

As another surprise, Mr. Howland brought his guitar with him. We sit on a blanket in the abandoned barn, and Mr. Howland tells me he's going to teach me a song. I hold the beautiful guitar in my hands while he sits behind me, placing his fingers over mine. After about twenty minutes, I can't play a whole song, but I can play a G and a D chord without help. We pass a bottle of blackberry brandy back and forth.

"Sing me a song," I tell Mr. Howland.

He takes the guitar and sits with his back against the wall. I lie on the blanket and close my eyes. Mr. Howland sings

"Just Like Tom Thumb's Blues" by Bob Dylan. It begins to rain outside while he plays. After he finishes, he carefully leans the guitar against the wall and comes over to where I am lying.

Do you need to know what happened? Do you need to know about the part where things didn't work, the part where Mr. Howland got so upset that we almost called it off? Do you need to know about how, after we finally got it right, it hurt enough to bring tears to my eyes? You probably want to know the X-rated details, the stuff that I'm not going to tell you because nothing about what we did felt wrong or X-rated at all. I'll tell you this: I could hear the rain softly tapping the roof of the barn and could feel a cool, damp wind coming through the small window. I was nervous and happy, and so was Mr. Howland, even though I knew no one would have thought too much of us lying there breaking about every rule a person could break.

I touch his eyelids and we both laugh because we have actually done it. We are going to put Mr. Howland's Dracula Principle to the ultimate test. We'll see if it will work now that we have gone all the way. The only person who would know, who wouldn't be fooled, is my mother, and she is not here. There may be others. I don't know. There may be people out there who know when something is real and worthy of believing in even when everyone else is shaking their heads saying it couldn't be true.

As we drive home I decide to mark this day, May 9, on my calendar. I am now a different person than I was this morning, an older person. I am a secret cave that has finally been explored, a cave that has been waiting for a very long time to be discovered. I am that cave and Mr. Howland discovered me. He is Marco Polo or Amerigo Vespucci and I am a brand-new continent. What I have discovered is a place inside me I didn't even know existed. And there is nothing in this world to prepare you for that kind of discovery. And, believe me, it is good to know those places are there.

The Living Room

IF MY MOTHER HAD A ROOM, it would be the living room, except that no one ever goes in there. My mother made it into the kind of place that you should look into and not mess up. The only one brave enough to enter is my mother's dog, Kippy. Everything in the living room is light blue, even the border and the flowers on the Oriental rug. In the curio cabinet are small glass statues and marble eggs from Russia in various swirling colors. When my mother was here, the couch pillows were always puffed up to the perfect consistency, and I was constantly fighting an insane temptation to flop down and flatten them out. Now, the pillows are never disturbed. There is a desk in the living room with about twenty little drawers in it, and I like to go through those drawers sometimes to look for interesting artifacts. For the most part, there are playing cards and tallies for my mother's bridge club, but once I found three or four sympathy cards written to my parents about my brother's death. One of them, an off-white piece of stationery folded in half, looked like a woman probably wrote it and it said that she and her husband were praying for my parents. The letters were big and loopy and very neat. The last three words were "With deepest sympathy."

When I read that card, I pictured my brother sitting on the floor of a hotel room somewhere near Johns Hopkins University, where he was going to see his psychiatrist. In my imagination, he won't look at my parents and is rocking himself back and forth and hitting his hands against his face. He is not a real boy with real flesh and blood; he is more like a plastic doll. Still, he is much cuter than I ever was because he has blond hair and blue eyes. I picture him wearing red overalls and black-and-white saddle shoes. He looks normal from the outside, but something is terribly wrong. Inside, he is completely alone and he can't tell anyone what he is feeling. He is locked up inside his perfect-looking doll body, and he wants someone who feels the way he does to understand what is happening. But there is no one like him. I try to picture myself sitting next to him holding his hand. My mother is there, but she is afraid this is all her fault. She worries about who will take care of him when he grows up. I wish I could tell her I will take care of him, but I haven't even been born yet.

My Father's Room

THOUGH I AM OFFICIALLY A DIFFERENT PERSON, not being virginal anymore, my father is the same as always. He is sitting in his study working on a file from his law office. His is different from the other rooms in the house because he decorated it himself. He wanted it to be wood-paneled. A big and strange nature painting hangs on the wall. The entire painting is out of whack in terms of perspective. Mr. Howland would have a field day criticizing it—the chipmunk would be as tall as the pine tree if it were drawn to scale. My father also collects wood carvings of people who appear to be Chinese. The Chinese people carry wooden fishing poles and baskets. There is even a wooden totem pole with Chinese faces carved into it. God knows where he got that stuff; my mother sure didn't buy it. She has good taste, but my father is completely different. It is hard for me to imagine what he thinks when he looks at that totem pole and those miniature wooden Chinese people and those wooden squirrels and that crazy woodsy painting with the chipmunk and the purple clouds. For all I know, my father could secretly wish he was Chinese. Those figures don't make my father all nervous and cranky, the way he gets around me. I bet those statues make him feel peaceful, like he has his own magic kingdom where he rules everything—his personal secret spot where he can escape from me and my mother and Kippy. Tonight he is yelling at the New York Knicks. If my father could meet the coach of the New York Knicks, he would never run out of things to tell him. My father loves the Knicks so much that he even used to have season tickets to the games so that we wouldn't miss anything.

Our seats were way back in the blue section—farthest away from everything. We went to see the Knicks' home games most Tuesday nights and almost every Friday night for years. I brought Barbie whenever I was allowed and her parents said it was all right. We ate hot dogs and had cardboard cartons of chocolate and vanilla ice cream. Barbie and I watched the game, not really caring what was happening until the last five minutes or so, when everyone would stand up and begin cheering loudly if it was a close game. I liked the nicknames the players had, names like Clyde and Pearl.

When we would go to the games, we drove in my father's fancy car with a leathery smell that made me sick to my stomach. What I remember of my parents from those trips is looking at the backs of their heads. My father usually let us play a Beatles eight-track all the way to New York. Barbie and I sang along to "Fool on the Hill," our favorite song. We never got tired of that song, no matter how many times we played it. My mother didn't care too much about the Knicks, so we ate dinner in fancy restaurants like Mama Leone's and Luchow's and the Four Seasons in order to make the trip worthwhile for her. Once, when I was very young, before the days when I was allowed to bring a friend, we were in the Four Seasons. I asked my father for the cherry from his Manhattan and the waiter brought me a whole glass full of cherries. Sometimes, as we walked toward the parking garage, I held my father's hand and skipped so that I could keep up, pretending to limp when he limped. I hung there from his arm, letting my feet dangle above the sidewalk until he lowered me back down to the ground.

As I watch him reading in his study, it is difficult to imagine being small enough to be lifted off the ground by my father. He rarely looks up from his papers. My stomach has been feeling pretty awful since yesterday in the woods with Mr. Howland, but I don't want to tell my father because he might want me to have a checkup, which would reveal the fact that I am no longer the innocent child I once was. I dig my nails into my hands to stop worrying. My father sits, oblivious to my presence. Unlike me, he can concentrate his attention on his work, not distracted by the unusual world he has created around him.

Western Civilization

MY WESTERN CIVILIZATION TEACHER is by far the best-looking teacher in the school. I'm supposed to be taking science this year, but I almost failed Chemistry as a sophomore and my guidance counselor let me load up on humanities classes. Mr. Wallace is even handsomer than Mr. Howland. He has straight black hair and blue eyes and perfectly white teeth. Every girl in our class is in love with him, and every one of us would give anything to trade places with his wife, who he calls "the Fox." The Fox goes to the football and wrestling matches when Mr. Wallace is coaching, and she really is a fox. She resembles one of Charlie's Angels, the one played by Farrah Fawcett. It doesn't bother any of us that we don't learn anything in Western Civilization, because none of us are all that interested. Most days Mr. Wallace lets us have what he calls "student-oriented activity days," which means we can do our homework or talk or whatever.

Both Mr. Wallace and the teacher in the adjoining classroom are Vietnam veterans, but they couldn't have more opposing views of the war. Mr. Wallace rarely mentions Vietnam. He loves to talk about wrestling and, on occasion, demonstrates a move with a boy in the class who is on the team. One day he shoved the kid into the giant trash can in the hallway and broke his tooth. Mr. Wallace says his goal is to turn us into little Republicans. He hates Jimmy Carter and wants Ronald Reagan for our next president. To be honest, the only news I've heard about Reagan, aside from the fact that he was a movie star, is that he will overturn a woman's right to an abortion, and that seems pretty scary. Not that my goal in life is to have an abortion, but in the event I needed one, it would be pretty terrible not to have the choice.

Mr. Aniello, the teacher next door, is an entirely different story. One day back in the fall, we had to spend two whole days in Sociology learning about the life of his friend who died in the war in Vietnam. He even gave us a quiz on this guy. We had to know his dead friend's birthday and the day he died and the reasons why he signed up for the war. The students like Mr. Wallace better, and I think he has more influence on how we view the war because he isn't overly hung up on it. He makes it sound like it was fun sometimes. He did tell us that he never told his family or anything when he was coming home; he just showed up without any warning. Actually, if you think about it, World War II seems like it was a better war to fight. My father and other men his age seem fine, but no one I've met so far came back from Vietnam without some sort of problem. Even someone as perfect as Mr. Wallace.

The rest of the faculty, however, doesn't see Mr. Wallace's perfection. Mr. Howland calls him a moron, and Ms. Clewell rolls her eyes whenever we tell her what we think is a funny story from Western Civilization. She never directly calls him names, the way Mr. Howland does, because it almost seems that teachers are part of some secret society that doesn't really break ranks. Still, she will give a good eye roll if we relate an especially outrageous story about his class.

Ms. Clewell is the only adult in the school who really tries to *teach* us. I don't fully understand why Mr. Wallace, Mr. Howland, and most of my other teachers chose the profession. Still, while there are a bunch of faculty members who chose this career for reasons I don't understand, I am very glad they did end up here because school would be a whole lot less interesting without them.

Back to the Shrink

IT'S WEDNESDAY. I'm sitting in the waiting room at Dr. Chester's office. One of the true benefits of therapy is that I get to leave school early and still play in tennis matches, if we have one. There is potentially a lot to say, especially about the fact that I've had actual sex, but I'm planning not to say much of anything. Dr. Chester opens the door and holds it open. As I walk into the office, I make a stupid face knowing that he's behind me and can't see me. It is a serious place, this office, dark and paneled, with plaques and degrees framed on the walls. I sit across from the doctor and look at him, wondering if he can actually help people—if he has any power whatsoever. What good can come from me sitting here and telling him about the crazy stuff that has happened lately? Could I actually tell him about what happened in the woods with Mr. Howland? Why in the world would I want to become even more worried and guilty for doing the one thing I feel happy about lately? How could Dr. Chester understand how it felt to be lying under Mr. Howland? Would he understand that it was worth the painful parts? He wouldn't approve. There is no question about it.

"Hello," I say. I say hello because I've noticed something. Dr. Chester will not be the first one to talk. It must be part of the curriculum they teach in shrink school. Lesson 1—never be the first person to say hello. He would let me sit there in silence for the whole hour, I think.

"Hello," he says back.

"I can't think of anything to say," I tell him.

"All right," he says.

I sit there looking around at the walls and at the statues of creepy voodoo-looking people on the shelves. I wonder if my father would like to add these creatures to his collection. Actually, these statues look African, and he probably wouldn't like them all that much. Some of Dr. Chester's carvings even have boobs and skinny penises.

"How much does one of these sessions with you cost?" I ask.

"Is that important to you?" he asks.

"I'd like to know," I say.

"Ninety dollars."

"Holy moly," I say and whistle. "That's pretty steep."

"This time is valuable," he says.

My parents would never in a billion years hand over ninety dollars to me to spend how I wanted. So why are they spending the big bucks for this?

"Are you tired today?" I ask.

"Why? Do I seem tired?"

"I asked you first."

I am determined to beat him at his own game. What I want right now is to get into my car, smoke a cigarette, and listen to *Astral Weeks* very loud.

"You know what my father said to me?" I ask.

"No, what did he say?"

"He said that he wishes he could afford to be psychotic."

"He's expressing a wish," Dr. Chester says. "However, I am afraid he is misusing the word 'psychotic.' "

"He means crazy," I say. "He thinks I'm crazy. My mother, too. My dad thinks we are both crazy."

"Do you think you are crazy?"

"No," I answer. "I think *you* are crazy. Crazy like a fox."

He doesn't answer, not that I expect him to answer. I would like to find a way to ruffle his feathers. But he's tough. He can hold a bored and unimpressed expression on his face longer than anyone in the world, I think.

"Guess what?" I say.

"What?"

"I have this weird fear I'm going to get poisoned accidentally or that I'll swallow shards of glass without knowing it."

Although I am speaking in a joking and not serious way, the truth is that I do worry incessantly about being poisoned.

"Do you think that is going to happen?" he asks.

"It's possible," I say. "Anything is possible. Doesn't that scare you? Every time you take an aspirin you are potentially risking your life."

"Life is risky." He yawns. "Sometimes even the most careful people get wiped out."

I look at him. He said something funny. This is the first funny thing he has ever said to me, and it has made me like him better. I almost feel like talking some more. I'd like to ask him what he meant when he said my father was expressing a wish. I've never thought about my father having wishes, even if they are wishes to be psychotic. I wouldn't even mind talking about my mother or my brother or maybe even Mr. Howland, but I feel like I've had the upper hand with Dr. Chester and I don't want to blow it.

In the car I dig out my *Astral Weeks* tape, a tape not one of my friends will let me listen to when I am with them. I first heard Van Morrison at the house of a girl I was friends with back in ninth grade. Actually, we weren't great friends or anything—it was more that she was terrific at algebra and I wasn't. We'd sit in her room doing math homework, and through the wall I'd hear music—Van and Bob Dylan and post-Beatles John Lennon music. This girl would yell at her brother to turn it down—her taste in music didn't extend beyond AM radio. One day when she left me alone, I sneaked into her brother's room and wrote down the names of the first five albums I saw. That was how I got *Astral Weeks* and *Blood on the Tracks* and even a great record that I still listen to fairly often by a band called Leon Russell and the Shelter People. I hardly ever saw her brother—he was a senior at the time and he kept his door closed whenever I was around. Still, if it hadn't been for him, I might never have discovered the existence of those records.

A Close Call

AFTER MY SHRINK APPOINTMENT YESTERDAY, I played my worst tennis match of the year. I got beaten by a girl who wasn't very good. Mrs. Schwimmer shook her head at me, but she can't get mad because of my mother. The girl kept hitting junk at me, loopy lobs that made me want to kill the ball. Most of my shots went practically into the back fence. I knew the game was getting away from me, but I couldn't do anything about it. I kept hitting the ball as hard as I could until the match finally ended. Afterward, I told Mrs. Schwimmer that I would continue to play matches but that I'd have to miss practice for the next two weeks because I was needed at home. It was a lie, but I do think my father is getting closer to forcing the issue of a visit. Like everyone else, Mrs. Schwimmer gave me guilt-inducing sympathy and support.

The good thing about missing practice is that now I am free in the afternoon. Today, however, as I get into the car, Mr. Howland says he needs to make a quick stop at home.

"Wait," I say. "We're going to your house?"

"Yeah," he says. "Don't worry. Mother Dracula is working."

We drive in the direction opposite from the secret spot, out toward the mall. A few miles later, we pull into a gravel driveway. Mr. Howland's house is set back about fifty yards from the road. It resembles a house from a fairy tale—like the witch's house in Hansel and Gretel. The shutters on the windows could have been shaped by cookie cutters. Behind the house are woods.

"This is a funny house," I say.

"The mortgage isn't funny," Mr. Howland says.

When he opens the door, I sit there hoping that he doesn't think I'm going to go with him.

"Come on," he says.

"Come on where?"

"Don't be such a coward. You can see her car isn't here."

I don't know why I refuse to obey my inner voice, which is telling me to stay where I am, but I get out and follow him into the house, which is dark and smells of fresh-cut wood. There are the signs that he's been fixing things.

"I'll be right back," he says.

I wander around. An art studio looks like it was added on to the kitchen. The studio is filled with sketches done mostly with charcoal pencils. In the kitchen they have one of those old-fashioned black, potbellied stoves. On the counter is a small bowl filled with black licorice jelly beans, my least favorite flavor. Next to the studio is a set of stairs, and my curiosity gets the best of me. The stairs are wooden and worn, and the entire staircase tilts to the left; it's clearly not a part of the house that has been renovated. I begin to climb, trying not to think of a scary dream involving a staircase I used to have all the time when I was younger.

As I reach the top step, I realize I am seeing exactly what I came to see. The bed is unmade, and the room itself is decorated in a sort of artsy way. The pattern on the bedspread looks like one of the mosaic designs on Mr. Howland's pottery. Near the window, there is a screen made of wood and black cloth, much like the one Mr. Howland put on the window in his office, but it is larger, like you could get dressed behind it. I see Mr. Howland's jeans on the floor, but I don't see any of her clothes. On the night table is a gold wedding band. I think to look in the closet, but then I hear a sound that causes my heart to stop inside my chest for a second. I look outside. Pulling up next to Mr. Howland's car is her bright yellow Trans Am. I hear Mr. Howland's footsteps running toward the kitchen and then him yelling, "Where the hell are you?"

"I'll hide," I holler back.

I scoot under the bed. It is clear that the Howlands don't have a maid because I am covered with dust bunnies and breathing in what seems like enough dust to fill a vacuum bag. I feel claustrophobic, and unless I turn my head to the side, the bottom of the box spring touches my nose. Next to my face is a pencil stub, a pair of Mr. Howland's boxer shorts, and a single black jelly bean.

"What are you doing home?" Mr. Howland asks his wife.

They are at the bottom of the stairs. Every word is loud and clear.

"I forgot a file," Mrs. Howland says.

I figure that, if God exists, she won't come upstairs. If he doesn't, then she will. I hear her feet trotting up the steps and I hold my breath. She is wearing older woman shoes, brown sling-back pumps with a high heel. It amazes me that she can walk without falling down. She walks quickly past the room I'm in and into the room next door. She stays there for a minute or two and then goes back down the stairs. My heart is banging so loudly in my chest that I am surprised she doesn't hear it and drag me out from under her bed.

"Are you going to finish the walls in the living room?" she calls to Mr. Howland.

"I don't know," he yells back. "We're past the extension on the taxes. We need to get those out by the end of next week."

This conversation seems pretty mundane to me. Eventually, the front door slams; the muffled sound of a car door follows. Last, she revs up the engine, gravel crunching as she drives away. I slide out from under that bed, trying to get some of the dust off of me.

"What are you doing upstairs?" Mr. Howland calls to me.

"Hiding," I say.

"Jesus H. Christ," Mr. Howland says. "Let's get the hell out of here."

Before I go downstairs I pull open the closet door and discover a pile of trophies in a cardboard box. His wife was not exaggerating—there must be about twenty of them. I am even more impressed, because now I know that not only is Mr. Howland a great artist but he was a terrific athlete. Hanging over the bed, I see a framed print I hadn't noticed earlier. It is a painting of a man's face behind what appear to be the bars of a jail cell. Underneath the picture in bold capital letters it says, "AT THIRTY-FIVE PAUL GAUGUIN WAS WORKING IN A BANK. IT IS NEVER TOO LATE."

We don't talk about any of what happened as we drive out toward the secret spot. I don't care much about their taxes or their renovations, but I did want to see more of the house. I wanted to see their clothes and examine the football trophies, and I wanted to see what kind of food was in the refrigerator. Mr. Howland dragged me out before I had the chance to investigate much of anything.

Later, as we lie in the barn, I am studying the caps on Mr. Howland's teeth, the ones I noticed when he and Patty's mother were drunk and laughing at everything.

"Your teeth must be worth about a million dollars," I say.

"What can I say?" he says. "I'm rich with rottenness."

He pulls me toward him to kiss me, but I won't let him.

"I could steal your teeth one at a time and put myself through college," I tell him. "If only I had some chloroform."

He's not paying attention to anything I say. His only desire is to kiss me. This is one of those times where I suspect that Mr. Howland and I are perverts. Who else but a couple of perverts would do this? Who else but perverts would go to a gingerbread house and then drive in an old BMW through one hundred feet of pricker bushes to get to a clearing? Who would come to this place to be naked and drink brandy out of the bottle and have sex in an abandoned barn? Not to mention the fact that I'm seventeen and he is thirty-two and has a wife who is a paralegal. And I've got a father who might secretly wish to be Chinese for all I know. And a mother who could die without me ever visiting her. There is no other explanation. We are perverts.

While Mr. Howland is folding up the blanket, he begins to cry. It happens suddenly. I am lying still, feeling the cool breeze blow across my naked skin, raising the hair on my arms a tiny bit—not the way it does when you have chills or goose bumps but the way it does when you get out of the ocean on a sunny day. I am not accustomed to seeing people cry.

"What's wrong?" I ask.

"I love you," he says.

"I love you, too," I say.

Whenever Mr. Howland tells me he loves me, I want to pause time and make sure that I'm not in a fantasy. His "I love you" is so much better than mine. I'm not used to saying those words, so when I do, they sound fake to me, like I'm on a soap opera.

"What are we going to do?" he asks. He wipes his eyes with his sleeve.

"Are we going home?" I ask.

He's got tears running down his cheeks. They are pouring out of his eyes.

"Listen," he says. "I'm asking you what we are going to do. Do you have any idea what it is I'm asking you?"

I sit there silently.

"Don't you think I wonder what I have done here, Edna? Can't you see that I've got all my eggs in one basket?"

I am the basket. I am carrying all of Mr. Howland's eggs.

"I'm putting everything on the line here," he says.

He's looking at me like he wants me to say things, reassuring things, but there are no words because my emotions are malfunctioning. I'd like to tell him how much he can trust me to carry the eggs and not break them. But I've lied so much to my parents and my teachers and Dr. Chester that I don't know how to sound like I'm telling the truth. I don't want Mr. Howland to be crying because of me.

"Are you sure you love me?" he asks.

"Of course I do," I say. "You are my Mr. Handsome."

I think this will help, but Mr. Howland cries even harder. Sometimes I make up nicknames when I am nervous. Despite the fact that I am pretty confused and tongue-tied, I can honestly say that I do love Mr. Howland. I think about him all the time and I'm only truly happy when he is with me. Isn't that love? I hold Mr. Howland's beautiful hands, which aside from his sandy hair and square jaw might be his best feature. They are large and strong-looking, like my father's hands except without the bulgy veins and too-long fingernails. I remember pressing the biggest vein in my father's hand once, trying to push it back into his skin. That vein was thick and blue and ran between his thumb and forefinger. Every time I pushed it, it would reappear just as blue and thick. My father also has a big mole on his right cheek, a mole almost as big as a large pea. I used to pretend that his mole could talk. I look at Mr. Howland. For as much success as I am having making Mr. Howland feel better, I might as well be talking to that mole.

"Are you okay?" I ask.

"I don't know," he says.

"You don't know what?" I ask. I can feel dread rising up through my body. Losing Mr. Howland is not something I want to contemplate. I can't really say it to him, but he is keeping me happy.

"Don't you see?" he asks. He asks as though I can't possibly be so stupid as not to see. "I love you."

"I know," I say. "You said that already." But I don't see. I really don't. I don't see why he is so upset about everything. I have never been happier in my life than I am now with Mr. Howland.

We drive away, out of the secret spot, the prickers scraping the sides of the car as we pull onto the road. Mr. Howland rests his hand on my knee when he isn't shifting. I think of a vocabulary word from English class. The word is "ominous," and I can't get it out of my head. The day was ominous.

"I feel ominous," I tell Mr. Howland.

He squeezes my knee and continues on down the road.

The Gold Chair

EVER SINCE MY MOTHER LEFT for the hospital, Kippy won't move out of the gold chair next to her bed. At first it wasn't a big deal, but now she is losing weight and she's hardly eating or drinking. You see, Kippy loves my mother more than anything in the world. She follows her everywhere. Until she got sick, my mother made Mighty Dog hamburgers in the frying pan for Kippy's dinner each night. To be honest, they smelled pretty good. She added eggs and salt and sometimes a slice of American cheese. Kippy never let my mother out of her sight.

I used to be like Kippy. I even dropped out of Lincoln Nursery School because I liked being with my mother better than with the screechy-voiced lady who ran the school. Back then, I didn't like my mother to be beyond the reach of my voice. If I was in the tub, I'd call out every few minutes just to hear her answer. If I was playing Monopoly in the den with Sucan, I'd wander out to the living room to make sure my mom was still around. There was one day when I was five years old that I couldn't find her. I stood in front of the window screaming and screaming for her until she came back. She'd only walked over to the neighbors' for a minute.

My father doesn't know what to do about Kippy. Kippy doesn't really like my dad very much, and he doesn't want to upset my mother by telling her that Kippy isn't eating. The other day when I got home from school, I went in and petted Kippy for a few minutes even though she isn't too crazy about me either. The cleaning lady feeds her from a spoon. I'd try cooking up one of those special Mighty Dog burgers, but I've never made anything on the stove. The only cooking experience I have ever had has not left me inclined to try again. Back when I was a Girl Scout, each member of my troop had to enter a bake-off. At the last possible moment, as it was becoming clear that I would be arriving at our troop meeting with nothing, my mother whipped up some corn-flake macaroons. Naturally, they won the contest, and I moved forward into a district level bake-off. I had to wear my Girl Scout dress with the sash and show up at a home economics classroom at the high school, where I was to prepare my prizewinning recipe right there in front of a panel of judges. My mother had run through the steps of the recipe with me the night before, but none of the information stuck and I had no real idea how to make cornflake macaroons.

There is a photograph of me to commemorate this disaster. In the photo, I am holding a pan of burnt-looking cookies for the camera; my uniform, including the sash, is coated with flour and the remnants of macaroons. Though I am smiling, it is clearly a smile more of fear and fakery than of happiness. The part of the story where the macaroons were prepared has been blocked out of my mind. Needless to say, I didn't make it further in the competition. That was my first and last year of Girl Scouts.

Since my mother has been away, her friends have brought food, but I haven't been overly hungry myself.

Another Night at the Pharmacy

I AM STANDING AT MY REGISTER waiting for the perfect moment to shove two packs of cigarettes into my purse when who walks in the door but Mr. Howland. I'd had a panicky feeling lately that he was sort of avoiding me because of the weird stuff in the car the other day, but here he is. He is wearing what he would describe as a shit-eating grin and browsing around with his hands in the pockets of his jeans as if he is an ordinary customer, except he's wearing his Ray-Ban sunglasses. While we do have an unusual climate in here, it isn't sunny. He waves to me, and I wave back. Emory buzzes, and I go to the pharmacy counter.

"Who in the world is that?" Emory asks.

"A guy I know."

Besides looking like Elvis and being drunk most of the time, Emory is spookily psychic.

"You want me to get rid of him? He looks like a creep." Emory emphasizes the word "creep." He exaggerates his slight Southern accent, probably so that he can better resemble Elvis.

"That's okay," I tell him. "I'm okay."

I return to my register, and Mr. Howland comes up with a bottle of saline solution. As far as I know, he doesn't wear contacts. Maybe his wife does. It feels wrong for him to be here in a way I can't explain.

"Can you meet me tonight at eight?" he asks. "Witchy-Poo is going out." He always calls his wife some dumb name.

"At the church?" I ask. "I get out of here at seven."

It seems weird that neither one of us has plans on a Friday night.

"I'll meet you there at eight," he says.

I ring up his saline solution and ask him if he'd like a bag.

"Keep working hard," he says, "or hardly working."

I smile and don't give him a bag. I hate puns or whatever it was he said. Whenever Mr. Howland says something stupid like that, I wonder if I even love him. The phone buzzes and I pick up. It's Emory.

"Hey, Smiley," he says.

"What is it, Emory?"

"How's your friend?" After he asks, he laughs and laughs. "Now where in God's name did you make a friend like that?"

"Did you want something?" I ask.

"I'm low on V8," Emory says. "Take twenty out of the register."

So I walk down the row of stores in the strip mall past the nail salon and the doctor's office to the Cumberland Farms, where I get Emory a six-pack of V8 and myself a Coke. On my way out I see Mr. Howland's car pulling onto the highway, and his head looks too big through the window. I don't know why I never noticed before how big his head looks when he is driving. It could be his hair. I put the change in my pocket because I know that Emory won't remember to ask for it and I won't put it back in the register.

A Quick Stop at Home

AT HOME I RUN UPSTAIRS without looking for my father and put a record on my new stereo that I paid for with money both earned and stolen from Emory. I listen to "Babe I'm Gonna Leave You" by Led Zeppelin while I search for a comb. I'm supposed to be writing a short paper expressing my opinion on the Iranian hostage crisis for Western Civ, but I'm banking on the fact that Mr. Wallace will forget to collect it. There is barely enough time for me to smoke a cigarette before I head back to the church; I have the music turned up pretty loud, and I'm hanging my head out my bedroom window to keep the air clear. What I really want is to listen to "Madame George" off *Astral Weeks* before I leave, but I don't have enough time. I change into jeans and a T-shirt and go downstairs.

I walk through the family room toward my father's office and I hear the sound of gunfire from his favorite program, *G.I. Diary*. For a moment I consider going in there and talking to him, but then I realize I am late, I might still smell like smoke, and my father would have yet another reason to be disappointed in me. For some reason I've been thinking about Peter Robin a lot lately. I can see the whole thing so clearly in my mind—my father sitting on the side of my bed and me smaller than I can imagine myself being.

Back to the Secret Spot

I LEAVE THE HOUSE without saying anything to my father. Inside the car, I light another cigarette and roll down the window. I'm blasting "Monkey Man" by the Rolling Stones. It's not far to the church and Mr. Howland. It is easy to keep my mind clear by focusing on the sound of music and the wind. He's not there yet when I pull into the parking lot, so I park where I can look at the oncoming row of headlights. The BMW's are like a cat's eyes. I am starting to panic, worrying that he won't come, and a big black sinking feeling is rising inside my stomach. Then I see the cat's eyes coming toward me and my spirits lift.

Mr. Howland looks handsome as usual in his white

button-down shirt and jeans. He wears scuffed-up penny loafers on his handsome feet, and his head doesn't look nearly as big as it did in the pharmacy parking lot.

"I missed you, you little nut," he says.

"I missed you, you big nut," I answer.

"Ready for takeoff?" he says.

"Rodger Dodger," I say.

We leave my car not under the streetlight but in a dark and inconspicuous area of the parking lot. It is pretty warm outside and coincidentally Mr. Howland has the Rolling Stones playing in the tape deck and this is what I think happiness is. It is not sitting in your room doing homework and trying to get an A or doing dishes to make your father who doesn't talk think you are a good daughter. And it is not visiting your mother in the hospital where she could be dying for all you know. It is this. It is riding in the car with the windows down on a warm night knowing that soon your clothes will be off and you will be held closely by a clean-smelling, handsome man on a semisoft blanket. It is feeling good while doing something wrong at the same time. It is being where no one would think to look for you. Happiness used to be lying under my quilt listening to stories about Peter Robin, but those times went away and I suspect it wasn't my fault. As far as what happiness will be later on, I really can't say.

We pull through a thick clump of pricker bushes into the clearing, or what Mr. Howland thought was the clearing, but we've made a mistake and the car bottoms out in a ditch—a culvert—something pretty deep, and Mr. Howland starts cursing like a madman.

"Shit, piss, and corruption," he yells.

Our wheels are spinning. They are spinning so fast that they make a whizzing and whining sound. I am pretty sure that being stuck means we are truly screwed. This is the opposite of happiness. This is your buzz killed as you discover that you are about to be caught doing something both illegal and morally wrong. This is picturing a tow truck with your father in the passenger seat pulling up to where you are standing next to a BMW in the ditch with your Ceramics teacher as your father looks at you like it is impossible that you are the same person who used to be small and listen to stories about Peter Robin.

Mr. Howland gets out of the car, slams the door, and stands outside looking at the tire.

"Get in the driver's seat," he orders.

"What for?" I yell. My trust for his ideas and theories is diminishing the longer we are stuck.

"You need to rock the car," he says. "I'll push."

There is a trace of panic in his voice. I climb over the stick shift into Mr. Howland's seat. I see him through the windshield, standing in front of the car with his arms on the hood, spookily illuminated by the headlights. He looks like the maniac from the scary stories you tell around a campfire. He gives me the signal to begin rocking.

"You'll wreck your penny loafers," I yell.

"First and then reverse," he yells. "I want to go backwards."

Mr. Howland puts our sex blanket under the tires for traction. I'm rocking and getting into an impressive rhythm when my foot slips off the clutch and the car lunges forward. Mr. Howland dives to the side as the car springs forward, almost as if the car itself was trying to kill him. I scream pretty loud as my foot finds the brake.

"Jesus H. Christ, Edna," I hear from the darkness.

Mr. Howland has a few scratches on his face, and there are burrs and prickers stuck in his hair and on the sleeves of his shirt. There is sandy dirt caked on his pants and shoes. But the good news is that we are free. I try to pick the stickers and burrs out of his hair as Mr. Howland gets into the driver's seat and guides the car out of the false secret spot— the trap. When we are both sure that we are safe, we start laughing even though almost killing someone isn't that funny. Mr. Howland gets the blanket and then drives about fifty yards down the road until we see the entrance to the real secret spot, though there isn't much time now. He's pretending to be out at a bar and I can't stay out too late. We have a little while to be together, but all we can do is laugh and feel scared about what almost happened.

"What did you do?" he asks. "I was pushing so that we'd go backwards and out."

"I'm not sure," I tell him. "I think my foot slipped."

On the way home, we always pass a house that catches my eye. The house is so small it looks like it has one room.

When it is daylight, you can see toys scattered across the lawn, including a Big Wheel and a red plastic fire truck. There is a car with no wheels balanced on cinder blocks. The hood is up and it looks like someone is trying to repair it, but my guess is the car will never be fixed. It is probably the person who lives there trying to find a way to pass the time—to keep trying to fix a car that can't be fixed. I must admit to worrying about the kids who live in that house and play with the broken-looking toys. My mother once helped out at a church bazaar and she let me come along. There were long tables where people were selling cookies and homemade pot holders and other stuff to raise money for the church. I only had two dollars, and with that small amount of money I bought two stuffed animals, a board game, and a car for my Barbie doll. When I got home, both of the board games were missing pieces, the stuffed bear had weird bald spots that I hadn't noticed, and the Barbie car was missing the steering wheel. There was something wrong with every one of those toys. That is what I think of when I see the toys scattered around that yard—you have a pretty good idea that something is wrong with each and every one of them. This time I am waiting for the cinder-block house. I point to it as we pass. It's almost too dark to see, but I bet Mr. Howland knows which house I'm talking about.

"How would you like to live in *that* house?" I ask.

"I'd like to get rid of the house I have," he says.

It is becoming clear to me there is no easy answer to the question of how and why one family lives in a broken-down house like that one while my father and I share such a huge house, a house so big we don't even see each other most of the time. Or why one person spends his free time trying to fix a car up on cinder blocks while another person watches *G.I. Diary*.

Mr. Howland and I say goodbye. We kiss, and he hugs my head against his chest, where there are still a few remaining remnants of the burrs. His hands pull me close, and I feel the love coming through him and into me. It is a feeling you don't get very often, especially when your mother is in the hospital. It is the main reason I won't tell Dr. Chester about Mr. Howland or any of this, because I am pretty certain he would not understand—I'm not sure there are many people who would understand anything about it. Dr. Chester would probably call the pervert police and make me stay in counseling for the rest of my stupid life. I'd be trapped in some room with a bored-looking bald guy in a poplin suit asking questions until I figured out the answers that would make him go away.

The Gold Chair Empty

MY FATHER HAD TO TAKE KIPPY to the vet because the cleaning lady can't get her to eat anymore. He is probably pissed because Kippy always gets sick and it costs a fortune to fix her. Kippy and I have never been best friends, but I felt pretty bad when I saw my father trying to pry her off that gold chair. She is still convinced my mother is coming back. When I felt her nose, it was hot and dry, and even I know that a dry nose is a bad sign for a little dog. My father carried her out to the car wrapped in a blanket. He said not to tell my mother Kippy was sick, but I don't talk to her so he doesn't need to worry.

A Party at Patty's House

THE NEXT NIGHT Patty's mother is going to see a play in New York, so Patty invited Barbie and me over to hang out. As Barbie and I have grown apart, Patty and I have gotten closer. The most obvious reason is that Patty and I have three classes together this year. The tough part is that my family is pretty well off, but since Patty's dad died, her mom has to watch money carefully. She told Patty that even though her heart might be set on Holy Cross or even Yale, she'll probably have to take a scholarship from Rutgers. As it is, Patty has to work at Burger Chef to save money. Another point of contention between us is that while I seem to have a charmed life when it comes to not getting busted for things, Patty gets caught even when *I'm* the culprit. Her mother found *my* cigarettes under Patty's bed and Patty took the blame. I was too much of a coward to confess. The worst part is that Patty's mother keeps telling her she should be more like me.

I told Mr. Howland that we were going to be at Patty's tonight. I haven't been to Patty's house in over a month, since the night Mr. Howland and his wife were there. It's about eight o'clock, and we've been drinking screwdrivers since seven. On the way over here I told Barbie about Mr. Howland and me. It's gotten to the point where someone needs to know, and I knew that Barbie would be trustworthy. We have a long history together, especially when it comes to secrets. Barbie is the nicest person I know. Even when we were in elementary school and I bossed her around and made her play games I invented, she was always nice. We had sleepovers every Friday when we were in fourth grade and made up songs about how much we hated confirmation class. Sometimes we played with our Barbie dolls until midnight. Whenever I do see her, I still feel like we're best friends.

"Guess what?" I said.

I was driving the Triumph TR7. Barbie hasn't really gotten a chance to ride in it, so she wanted me to pick her up even though she lives quite close to Patty.

"What?" she asked.

"I'm having an affair."

As I mentioned earlier, one of our favorite things to do when we were young was to record our own soap opera. We called it "All My People." I did the men's voices and Barbie did the women's. Affairs were a pretty common occurrence on our soap opera.

"Get out," she said.

"No, really."

She already knew a bit about Mr. Howland and me from

seeing us together at school. Back in March, I told her I had a crush on him.

"You really did it?" she asked.

"Yup," I answered.

The look on her face let me know she thought the whole thing was pretty exciting.

"I suspected this," she said. "Did you tell Patty?"

"No way," I answered.

"Patty will flip out," she said. "She wants him."

"I know. So does her mother."

We both laughed like we were back in my room with the tape recorder going making up this story. Barbie kept laughing.

"This is insane," she said. "How did it happen?"

"He told me to give him a hickey on his birthday."

"A hickey? Did you do it?"

"Yeah, I sucked his neck."

She and I both cracked up. She liked that I was telling her and that I hadn't told Patty. Barbie knows about how Patty thinks she isn't too smart. But Barbie also knows she is about a thousand times more popular and better-looking than Patty will ever be, at least in high school.

"Have you actually had sex with him?" she asked.

I nodded my head. "Numerous times."

"Holy crap," she said. "You are having an affair."

"I know."

"Was it fun?"

"It felt like getting pried open with a crowbar," I told her.

"Oh, my God," she said. "That's why I keep telling Billy we need to wait. I heard it's seriously painful."

"It only hurts for a few minutes. Then it's extremely weird."

"How am I going to act around him?"

"Pretend you don't know anything," I instructed her.

"I'm going to start laughing," she said.

"Then he'll know you know," I told her.

"Oh, my God."

That was right before we pulled into Patty's driveway. Now we are sitting around the table drinking screwdrivers. After we listen to the Boss for a while, Patty puts on her Eddie Money record, and we're dancing around the room holding pretend microphones and singing "Two Tickets to Paradise" when we start screaming because we see someone standing outside the picture window. After about one second of fear and confusion, I realize it is Mr. Howland and that he has been watching us dance. Barbie gets so scared that she throws her drink at the window. It hits the floor and orange juice spills on the carpet. We start laughing, and I can see that Patty is pretty excited. She might even imagine Mr. Howland has come over to see her—that he has been secretly in love with her all along. I act like it doesn't mean anything to me that he's there. Barbie behaves like a person on laughing gas. She is giggling like a lunatic.

Mr. Howland comes through the front door and looks around.

"What happened here?" he wants to know.

"You frightened us," Barbie responds. "I threw my drink." She is still giggling.

Mr. Howland shakes his head. He is amused by Barbie. In a way, I sort of envy that Barbie can just be herself and not have the complications that come with being me. Mr. Howland is a grown-up to her, and she is a regular teenager in his eyes. It is difficult to believe that only one night ago I almost killed him with his own car.

He sits down at the table, and Patty asks him if he wants something to drink. I'm waiting for him to do his Dracula imitation where he says, "I don't drrrink wine," but he doesn't. It is getting to the point where I can often predict what he is going to say. We sit down around him and start talking about school.

"I'm on my way to the mall to get a haircut," Mr. Howland says. "But I'm afraid that I'll lose all my strength if they shear my mane." He shakes his thick blond hair.

"Where's Melinda?" Patty asks.

Patty is allowed to call both Mr. Howland and his wife by their first names because her mother is a teacher.

He ignores her question. "Why don't you girls cut my hair?" he invites. "First you have to wash it, though. I love getting my hair washed." He gives me a look like he wants me to wash his hair, and I have to admit I like the idea.

Right away, it is clear that Patty sees herself as in charge of this whole situation. She shoves Barbie and me out of the way, wraps a dish towel around Mr. Howland's neck, and leads him to the sink. I want to kick her in the ass while she's washing his hair. He keeps laughing and making stupid jokes. Finally, when she is done, she makes him sit in a kitchen chair, and despite her knowing I've cut people's hair before, she won't let me near him and insists on doing it herself. I think she would have stabbed me if I kept trying.

Mr. Howland is sitting on a chair in the middle of Patty's small kitchen, and no matter what he says, he looks nervous as hell. I think he likes the way he looks. He keeps telling Patty not to cut too much. I'm pacing around because I can see how much Patty is enjoying this, having maximum power over Mr. Howland with me safely out of the way. I keep making wisecracks that aren't even necessarily funny. Barbie is still on laughing gas. It's clear she can't get over the knowledge that Mr. Howland and I had sex. Finally, Patty starts blow-drying his hair, and you can hardly tell that she cut it. Maybe it looks a bit shorter on top. I suspect Patty would like to pick up his hair and stick it in her diary or something, but I sweep it up with a dustpan and throw it in the garbage thinking, Ha-ha, your big moment is over.

After the haircut, Patty decides to go down to the 7-Eleven for cigarettes with Barbie, and I can't believe our good fortune. As soon as they are out the door, Mr. Howland grabs me and starts kissing me and squeezing me—I can tell that he is quite excited, and I wonder if it has something to do with the fact that we are in the home of the chairman of the English Department. We are sort of slow-dancing; the record plays a slowish Rolling Stones tune called "Till the Next Goodbye," and his hair smells good from the Wella Balsam shampoo that Patty used on him. It's funny, and you probably won't believe me, but as we were dancing I had this feeling I was watching us from the ceiling way over in the corner. And I was thinking, Uh-oh, something bad is going to happen.

The door flies open, and Patty comes charging into the room like a bull. Mr. Howland is the matador and he steps aside, but he has no cape; there is no Dracula Principle or diversion to make Patty forget what she just saw. Barbie told me later that Patty suspected us and made up the story about going for cigarettes so that she could look through the window. Barbie tried to keep her away, but Patty is strong and she shook Barbie off. Patty crawled into the bush by the window and watched everything—the kissing, the hugging, and even the butt squeezing. Every one of her suspicions was confirmed. She didn't say anything to Barbie, she just bolted for the door.

I'll tell you this: even my mother isn't as powerful as Patty. Patty starts yelling at us, something about using her and her mother and other stuff, but my efforts to tune her out are useless in the face of the fear she instills. Mr. Howland does look alarmed—he grabs his jacket and leaves. Barbie follows him out, to walk home, I figure.

I'm supposed to sleep over at Patty's, and I don't want to risk driving all the way out to my house in the stressed-out, drunken condition I'm in. I think she likes the fact that I am trapped because she can be as mean as she wants and there is nothing I can do, having been caught red-handed.

"You both make me sick," Patty yells at me.

"And don't think you are going to use me to see each other," she adds, almost spitting with fury. She is so mean that I have to go to the bathroom and throw up. A benefit of being nervous enough to vomit is that afterward I feel well enough to lie down and fall asleep on the couch without a blanket. Later, in what feels like the middle of the night, I hear Patty's mother trying to get her key into the lock on the door. It takes her quite a few tries. She mumbles a curse when she trips over my shoes as she walks past me toward her bedroom, but she doesn't seem aware that I am lying there in my clothes.

When I wake up, it is still very early and no one else is awake. The sky outside the picture window is a grayish color streaked with red. I can see the stain on the rug where Barbie threw her drink. On my way through the kitchen, I accidentally kick over the garbage pail, and I see small clumps of Mr. Howland's curly hair fly down to the floor.

The Gold Chair, Again

It is Sunday morning, and my father has gone to church. I am sitting in the gold chair by my mother's bed, where the imprint of Kippy was still visible before I took her place. Sitting here, I see clearly that we haven't really lived in this house long enough for it to feel like home. My father's side of the bed is unmade.

I think I mentioned this already, but when I was about

four or five years old, I had a recurring nightmare. I'd be going visiting with my mother and we'd pull up in front of a big, scary house that looked sort of like Lincoln Nursery School, the school I'd begged to quit. In the dream, my mother is taking me to this house so she can have coffee with the female ghoul who lives there. As she and the ghoul sit down to chat, I go on a little exploratory mission. There is a long, winding, narrow staircase I start to climb. As soon as I get to about the third step, I begin to feel the presence of an invisible form next to me. With each step, it is as though the creature is getting stronger by draining the life from me. With each step, I see myself vanishing, becoming less and less visible, as the monster becomes brighter and more defined. I'm terrified, but I can't stop climbing. By the time I reach the top of the stairs, I sense that this being has drained most of my life and energy into itself, that it has tricked me. As soon as I realize the extreme danger I am in, I begin to fall back down the stairs, and then I wake up.

There was no variation in that dream. I never once made it to the top, and never once did the creature succeed in taking every drop of life from me. The only things I could see were that he was glowing and that he had black hair. I'd wake up drenched in sweat. Fully awake, I'd bolt out of bed, look both ways down the hall, and then tear down into my parents' bedroom, where I would stand over my sleeping mother like a child ghoul. No one had to say one word. Aware of my spooky presence, she'd poke my father in the back, and he would get up, take his pillow, and head out to the couch in the living room. I got to crawl in next to my mother, into the already warm spot my father left behind.

The whole nightmare thing got so bad I developed a special ritual that my mother performed with me at night. It went like this:

Am I going to have a dream?

No.

A nightmare?

No.

Promise?

Yes.

Swear?

Yes.

Solid gold guarantee?

Yes.

Everything beautiful in the world?

Yes.

Our words never once prevented the life-sucking ghoul dream, yet I still made us say them every single night. Once in a while my mother tried to shorten it by saying, "No, no, yes, yes, yes, yes," before I'd even asked the questions. I refused to let her get away with it.

Thinking it over, I feel sort of guilty for making my father leave his own bed every night, and I'm not too sure I'd do the same for my own ghouly kid. But the truth is I needed my mother to say those words, those exact words, before I could sleep. My mother tried to teach me a replacement prayer once. It was the prayer that begins, "Now I lay me down to sleep." For me, the problem with that prayer came later, when you are supposed to say, "And if I die before I wake." In my opinion, the entire point of a prayer is to ensure that you don't die before you wake, so why even say such a thing? As you can see, my personal prayer had no mention of dying.

I get up on the bed, on my mother's side, and put on her little half-glasses and open a book, like she would do. I'm not going to read it or anything. I'm just doing an experiment. Her body is so much bigger and softer than mine, which is thin and bony and hard. I see my reflection in the television set; I don't look anything like her. My mother is actually quite beautiful. She resembles a TV mom, like Donna Reed. As I look at the reflection of myself, it strikes me how strange it is that I have not visited her and that I have not even been willing to talk to her on the phone. As I sit there in her glasses on her bed, the memory of sliding into the warm place left by my father after my nightmare returns, and I can feel the softness and the receding fear; never once did my mother yell at me to go back to my bed. Believe me, if I knew why I was so afraid to see her, I would tell you. But somehow it seems that I have been appointed to prevent something even *worse* than this from happening, and that my only recourse is to stay clear.

A bright light passes across the television screen, and I get a feeling like I'm disappearing, like I am sinking or drowning in feathers. I gasp and jump out of their bed. I start making up my father's side of the bed, just to be nice, but then I lose interest and put everything back where it was and leave.

Back to School

THERE IS NO QUESTION Patty is going to give me the cold shoulder at school. I am driving my car, worrying about what will happen when I see her, but then something entirely un-expected occurs. I hear a song on the radio that is completely unlike any other song I've ever heard. It is the kind of song I would never expect to hear on the radio. The song is about a girl named Roxanne, who is a prostitute, and a guy who is trying to save her. What is amazing is that not only does the song make me forget to worry about Patty but it really is a brand-new sound. After years of disco and completely un-original pop music, with only the Boss to admire, this is quite remarkable. It is funny, but things that are new and original always lift my spirits. Maybe it seems like an exagger-ation, but listening to this song with the wind blowing through my excellent car suggests something changing—like maybe the era of Donna Summer and Styx and REO Speed-wagon is finally over once and for all. That something new and better will take their place.

At lunch I decide not to tell Mr. Howland about the song, because my guess is that he will once again bring up the Bea-tles or the dead guy from the 1960s and will be reluctant to admit that something new can be as good as they were. I do tell him about the rest of the night at Patty's house, leaving out the part where I puked. His hamburger is sizzling away on the hot plate.

"Do you think she'll tell her mother?" I ask.

"I don't give a rat's ass," he says.

He's trying to be tough, but anyone could see that he's worried. The Dracula Bubble has burst. Smelling the cooking hamburger makes me feel stupid for not making myself a sandwich—the smell is driving me crazy. My lunch consists of a Coke and a bag of chips from the machine.

I hear "Sawyer Howland," and I know Patty's mom is standing in the doorway. She looks at me like she's going to order me to leave, but then she must remember that my mother has cancer and she lets it go. She coughs her little smoker's cough, rattly and deathly sounding. Her face changes, and now she's looking at me like the poor girl who has such a bad crush on her teacher that she can't even let him enjoy his lunch.

"What's shaking?" Mr. Howland says in a phony happy way.

"Can you and Melinda come to the house for dinner on Friday?" she asks. "Ron and Dave are coming."

Ron Hurly is the art teacher in the next room, and Dave McNamara is the librarian. Though both of them had wives at some point, most kids think they are in love with each other. Mr. Hurly rarely comes over to Mr. Howland's room. His class is for painting, and when I walk past I'm always surprised to see that his students are actually painting in there. The only time I've seen him outside of school was when Patty's mom had a party during Christmas break and the teachers got pretty wasted. Mr. Hurly was dancing solo to "MacArthur Park" by Donna Summer in Patty's living room, so completely drunk that he kept crashing into the wall. Patty and I were supposed to sleep at my house that night, but instead we hung around in town and sneaked over to look in the windows. The other teachers, including Mr. Howland, were drinking, but Mr. Hurly was by far the most fun to watch.

"I'll ask the Succubus," Mr. Howland says.

It's clear that Patty's mom isn't going anywhere, and I have to get to class anyway. If I go now, I might be on time for my next class for the first time in quite a while. As I get my stuff together, Patty's mom is acting all silly and flirty and coughing the death rattle and barely acknowledging my existence. I linger too long, and Mr. Howland writes me a pass without me having to ask because I'm going to be late again. Patty must not have told her mom. I guess we're safe. For the moment at least.

Deliveries

NOT BEING ABLE to go over to Patty's house and spy on Mr. Howland and his wife is fine with me. I've got to work anyway, and to tell you the truth, I'm not too excited about ever seeing Patty again. I get the feeling she's just beginning to realize that she's actually hated my guts all along. She is always bitching about how I get things I don't deserve and complaining about how lucky I am to have parents who can afford any college I want. Sadly, she is aware that I probably can't get into half the ones that she could. As I'm leaving the house, the phone rings and I run back to answer without thinking it could be my mother, but the person hangs up, something that has happened to me twice in the past two days.

It's a beautiful night, and I drive with the roof off over to the pharmacy, where it seems, if it is even possible, that Emory has the temperature set colder than normal. He calls me to the back, and I'm expecting to see black icicles hanging from his hair. When I get to the pharmacy zone, it's clear that Emory is pissed off about something.

"That son of a bitch claims our tennis balls are overpriced," Emory says.

He's talking about Dr. Goldstein's wife, one of Emory's girlfriends who comes in every now and then to secretly meet with him in the greeting card section and then complain loudly about the prices. Her husband is a hotshot plastic surgeon. She's right about the prices—they are completely ridiculous, and you'd need to be a moron to shop here. Every once in a while, we have a phony sale. Emory marks up everything in the store by 20 percent and then has his big 20-percent-off sale.

"Smiley," he says. He's got an evil look in his dark eyes. "I want you to take every goddamned can of tennis balls in this store and drop them on that bitch's doorstep." He whispers the word "bitch's" for special emphasis. He grabs a large box and comes down from behind the pharmacy counter, where it is strange to see that he is actually a big, strong guy—maybe six three with a good build. He's throwing six-dollar cans of tennis balls into the box, and despite the freezing temperature, the watery black streaks are rolling down his neck.

The box of balls fits into my car, which is a relief because I didn't really feel like driving Emory's big old death mobile. As I pull away, a few cans on my lap, past the strip mall's parking lot and onto the highway, I notice the sun is down but there is still light. Lined up outside the garden center across from the strip mall are stone statues of frogs and trolls and birdbaths that you might want to put in your garden. They are like cheerful gravestones. Every time I drive to the pharmacy from home I pass a graveyard, and it always scares me. When you think about it, death might not be half so scary if you could have a big stone frog with a walking stick and a top hat standing over you. I'd like a gnome in a pointed red hat strumming a guitar.

I go up the winding roads toward the superswanky houses—so swanky that you can't even see most of them. Emory drew me a map, so when I see 60 Edgewood Court, I pull up the long driveway and notice that the Goldsteins must be having some kind of cocktail party; Mercedeses and Beemers and other expensive cars that plastic surgeons and such can afford line the driveway. I go into high-speed mode, practically throwing the cans of tennis balls onto the doorstep before ringing the doorbell that they probably won't hear and getting the hell out of there.

Back at the store, Emory is sipping a V8 Bloody Mary

complete with celery stalk while Dale works on some complex-looking papers.

"What'd she say? Describe the look on her face," Emory says.

"They were having a party. I left them on the doorstep," I say.

"God damn it, Smiley, you are a coward." Emory takes a sip from his drink. "That creepy friend of yours was here," he says, and he laughs in a sinister way. "I told him you were out on a delivery, a long delivery," he says. Emory is assuming I don't want to see Mr. Howland, but I do. However, I don't want Emory to think it's important, so I just shrug like it's no big deal.

"Listen, Smiley," Emory says. "I hate to do this, but Vinnie Russo called and he needs some bandages delivered. He got attacked by some nut at the racetrack."

Emory is telling me this with a serious look on his face, but you can see he thinks it's funny.

"If you don't want to go, I'll send Dale over there," he says.

"I don't have a license," Dale says, barely looking up from the paper.

Emory knows I'll go. I take the pharmacy bag with the gauze, tape, alcohol, and bandages inside and once again head into the surrounding swank. The Russos' house is in the newer development, but the driveways are just as long as the Goldsteins'. At the gate, they have one of those black jockey statues, but someone has painted his face and hands white. Mr. Russo is standing at the top of his circular drive-way wearing a white oxford shirt untucked over his fat stomach. The weird part is that the shirt is covered with giant ink stains and blood splotches, like he's a human Rorschach test. He walks to my car.

"Some jerk-off attacked me with a pen," he says.

I don't even have to get out of the car—he takes the bag through the window and hands me a twenty-dollar tip.

"Tell Emory I said screw you," he says.

He's a pretty gruesome sight with the blood and the ink.

It's completely dark outside by the time I get back to the pharmacy, so the brightness and cold feel even more disorienting than normal. When Emory hears about the pen and that Vinnie Russo told me to say screw you, he's amused. Even Dale thinks it's kind of funny. We stand around the back counter talking about Mr. Russo and the pen and the tennis balls until the phone rings and Emory yells "Suicide Time" and Dale and I get ready to close up. Mr. Howland doesn't come back—no cat's eyes to be seen in the darkness of the parking lot.

A Trip to the Hospital

MY FATHER MAKES IT PRETTY CLEAR that I have to go to the hospital with him. It is the end of May, and since tennis season is over, I no longer have any valid or invalid excuses not to go and see my mother. I know which afternoons and evenings I am working at least a week in advance, and there is no chance my father would believe me if I told him that I am actually *helping* by not going to New York. Technically, my mother should have been home by now, but she had to have her hip replaced where the cancer attacked the bone, and there were some complications.

The night before we are to go I have a crazy dream. I dream my brother, Tommy, and Peter Robin and I are riding in the car together. None of us is driving, but that doesn't seem to be a problem. We go past the hill where in real life my father had let me shift gears, and we are on a long stretch of road that goes straight through the desert. I am looking at Tommy and waiting for him to say something because I want to hear him talk, but he doesn't. Peter Robin is sitting next to me, and he looks like a cross between a regular robin and a cartoon crow like Hekyll or Jekyll. Then I am all alone in the car, and the fact that no one is driving is suddenly a very big deal. The car is headed toward a cliff, and there is a woman dancing at the edge, making strange waving movements with her arms. I wake up a moment before I go over the edge.

I meet my father at his law office. Right there, behind my father's office, is the most beautiful tree I have ever seen. It is a magnolia tree, and the thick, soft-looking flowers are streaked white and purple. Here is another side to my father. He has filled his yard with rosebushes—white, red, yellow, and pink roses are blooming all over the place, and there, right next to the parking lot, is this incredible tree that makes you want to lie down and cover yourself with those satiny purple and white flowers. My father is a real nut for wildlife and most living things. Aside from *G.I. Diary* and the Knicks, he also watches any show about nature.

In the back I see Karl, a black guy who does random odd jobs for my father, stuff like watering the roses and getting coffee. He lives in the small garage behind my father's office, and he wears three coats no matter what the weather. It drives my mother crazy that he wears the shortest coat on top. My father took me into the garage one time because he wanted to get a mailbox from Karl. Karl isn't quite right in his mind, and he collects mailboxes among other things. There must have been about fifteen brand-new mailboxes in there as well as alarm clocks and about one hundred calendars. My father told me that Karl got hit by a bus when he was a little kid and that he isn't able to have a regular life. What doesn't make sense is why my father, who isn't exactly the friendliest man in the world, lets Karl live in his garage and even sit on the front porch of his law office whenever he feels like it. Karl waves to me, he always waves to me, and I wave back. Waving at Karl always reminds me that Karl once saved my father's office from being burglarized. The robber hit Karl over the head with a bat, but Karl didn't back down. He showed me the bloody-looking welt on his head right at the edge of his hairline.

"They hit me on the head," he repeated. It was clear that Karl was proud of having protected the office.

In my mind, I am trying to form a clear connection between the tree and the roses and Karl. Each one of those things tells me something important about my father, something he cannot tell me himself. They represent pieces of an impossible puzzle that I am pretty certain I will never solve. But I keep paying attention anyway. Beautiful roses and a black man wearing three coats who is willing to lay down his life for you must be significant clues.

My father emerges from his office. He looks tired; his hat is cocked to one side. I like how men from my father's generation wear hats to work. I wish Mr. Howland would start wearing hats. We get into my dad's Oldsmobile, the good car, leaving my car out in the parking lot under the magnolia tree. He doesn't say anything to me about the fact that it is the first time I'm going with him to see my mother. That is one good thing about my father. You can always count on him not to say anything because he doesn't really like to talk. He's like Mister Ed, he only talks when he has something to say. As we pull out of the driveway, I see Karl take a seat on the front porch, and I wave one more time.

Driving to New York, my father looks like he is about to say something, but he doesn't. I believe he may even be having a conversation with himself inside his head, but I couldn't say for sure. The reason I think this is that he is gesturing with his hand every so often—karate-chopping the air in a way that makes it look like he is telling an imaginary person something very important.

As we head north on the turnpike, I feel my stomach starting to seize up. When I was a little kid, I used to pretend to be sick about once a week so that I could stay home from school and be served peeled apples and watch *The Price Is Right*. But then, ironically, I did get a stomach problem that has troubled me on and off. Lately, I've noticed that every time I'm around my father, I get a pretty severe pain in my stomach. This pain is coming on top of my normal car sickness, and I'm trying not to double over in the seat. It's like there is an alien living in my stomach, moving around creating havoc with my intestines. I tell my father to pull over, and I puke all over the side of the turnpike while cars and tractor trailers are whizzing by so close that I don't understand how we haven't been crushed. My father doesn't say anything; he simply hands me his handkerchief and I wipe my face.

You might think puking would make me feel better, but it doesn't, and I won't go into the gory details of what happens next, but my father has to stop at this horribly seedy-looking motel where pimps and hookers and drug addicts go to find one another. I have to use the bathroom there because it is nothing short of an emergency. When I come out of the bathroom that I won't even describe, I am still sick and colorless, and my entire body is shaking like I have malaria. My father is standing there in the scary lobby with his hat still cocked to one side looking at me like I am the world's weakest girl and a massive disappointment—both being true, I realize.

Without discussing what happened, we get back on the turnpike headed south, and my stomach starts to calm down a bit as we get farther away from New York and my sick mother. Without any warning my father starts quizzing me about directions.

"If you look to your left, which direction would you be looking?" he asks.

The fact is that I have no sense of direction whatsoever. Because of the war, my father is obsessed with directions and with distance.

"West?" I guess wildly.

"No, not west," my father says.

"North?" I try.

"Where is the sun?" he asks. "You need to know where the sun is setting."

I have no idea what he is talking about. Red sky at night, sailor's delight, I think, but that gives me no help with directions. When my father gets like this, it is best to listen and not speak. My stomach is experiencing aftershocks that could escalate, so I know I've got to tune him out. He goes on about the East River and about the setting sun, and I'm not even sure he cares if I answer anymore. He keeps talking and talking, emphasizing how important it is to know directions. He's gesturing with his hand, karate-chopping, which confirms he was talking to himself the whole time we were driving toward New York. If he knew how my stomach felt, I'm pretty sure he would stop talking, but he doesn't. He never mentions my mother at all, which in a way makes things worse.

As we get to the road that leads to our house, I want to ask him something. I want to ask him what happened to Tommy. Instead, I ask, "How's Karl doing these days?"

My father disrupts his monologue to look at me in a way that makes me think he had forgotten I was even there.

"He's all right," he says. "About the same as always."

"Was he murdered?" I blurt out. "Did someone murder Tommy?"

My father keeps looking straight ahead. He is thinking about the question like there is nothing strange about my asking. He considers it as if he had been expecting some such question.

"Did someone tell you he was murdered?" he asks.

"Well," I say. "Barbie asked me about it once when we were kids."

"No one murdered Tommy," he says. "People didn't understand about him. It was a different time."

"How did he die then?" I ask.

We are very close to home now, and my stomach has momentarily calmed down.

"He drowned," my father says. "He drowned in Maine, in the ocean. He was making some progress. He was very smart."

"How do you know he was smart if he couldn't talk?"

"Oh, you could tell. He would have been very smart. I wish you could have known him. I wish we'd had more time with him."

"What happened to that psychiatrist?" I ask him.

My father shrugs and gets a pained look on his face. This might be the part that he really does not want to talk about. Surprisingly, it was clear he liked talking about Tommy. He is waiting for me to ask more questions, and I want to ask more questions. I want to know who was responsible. I want to know *exactly* how my father could tell Tommy was smart. But no words come out of my mouth. It is a relief, however; it is a bigger relief than I can say to know that no one killed him.

We pull into our driveway.

"Will you tell her I tried to come?" I ask.

"Why don't you call her?" he replies. "I'll dial the number for you."

"I can't right now," I say. "I'm sick."

He shrugs his shoulders and walks into the house, into his private room with his statues and creatures. By the time I get into the hallway, I can already hear the voice of the narrator from *G.I. Diary*, and I know that my mother and I are safe for the night.

Up in my room, I try to think of a new prayer to say, something that might help me fall asleep, but the only thing that comes to mind is the time my father made me go with him all the way back to Freehold to bring Karl a clock that he had left at our farm while doing yard work. Why would we drive five miles out of our way to bring someone something he didn't really need? I am wondering if my father was so nice to Karl because Karl couldn't say what it was he wanted, the way Tommy couldn't say what *he* wanted. Karl said he wanted a *clock*, but without being a psychiatrist, it is still easy to see that no one wants a clock that much. He must have liked something in particular about it—the way Kippy liked to have a clock in her bed when she was a puppy. Whatever it was, my father understood Karl wouldn't be all right without that clock.

My mind shifts gears and starts thinking about Mr. Howland again, about how he played the guitar that time at
Patty's house. He really had a great voice. I try to remember
the song about the woman in the lighthouse, but I have forgotten all but the beginning.

Tommy

TONIGHT I HAVE ANOTHER DREAM about Tommy. I am standing in a grassy field, and Tommy is sitting on a cloud high
above me wearing overalls and a straw hat and holding a fishing pole. I'm looking up at him, and he's looking at me from
where he sits in the sky. The cloud floats down, and he's sitting right next to me with his fishing pole, though we are
nowhere near any water.

"Can you hear me?" I ask him.

He nods his head yes, but he still doesn't say anything.
Then the cloud starts floating back up into the sky, and my
brother looks happy to be leaving the earth again.

Mrs. Howland at the Pharmacy

IT IS TUESDAY EVENING and one of those times when I am
standing behind my register staring off into space. I'm standing there surrounded by film and batteries and cartons of
cigarettes, not printing any losing lottery tickets for people

who look like they can't afford to buy them. The phone light is on—Emory is talking to someone and probably will be for hours. Dale is busy doing actual pharmacy work in the back, and there isn't one customer in the store. It would be a good moment to steal some film or cigarettes, but my thievery has not been giving me the same rush that it used to and I've been contemplating giving up cigarettes altogether. To pass the time, I start tossing Tic Tacs into the garbage pail that I've placed about five feet away—it is a game I made up. Because I've missed quite a few times, there are tiny white mints on the carpet surrounding the pail.

I am bent over picking up the errant Tic Tacs when Mrs. Howland, a.k.a. Melinda, comes walking into the store. She has a new haircut; her freshly frosted hair is layered, and she looks more stylish than she did the night at Patty's house. She doesn't look at me, but I can feel she is here to see me. Despite the cold, I am suddenly sweating like mad. Big wet circles are growing under my arms. My impulse is to crouch down and hide behind the counter, but that would be stupid, because as soon as she gets close enough she'll see me. There is no doubt that I am trapped. She pretends to be browsing for a while and then walks toward me.

"Well, what do you know?" she says. "It's my husband's favorite student."

She's standing in front of me with no merchandise, staring at me.

"Hey," I say. "How's it going?" I try to sound cheerful, but the sweating gives me away.

"Two packs of Newports," she says. "Please."

She's glaring at me with mockery, but I still am not sure that she knows anything about Mr. Howland and me. I have an active imagination.

I ring up the cigarettes. Before she walks out the door, she glances back like she might know, but she might not. She definitely doesn't look like she feels sorry for me for being the poor girl with a sick mother. She takes a step toward me. She looks like she is planning to say something that requires her complete concentration.

"How do you like my husband?" she asks.

She places a ton of emphasis on the word "husband," probably to drive home the point that I could have no idea of the significance of what a husband is, and the truth is I don't.

"He's a good teacher," I say.

She snorts like she thinks my answer is funny, but that snort is in no way anything like laughter.

"A good teacher," she says. "I'll bet." She snorts again.

I want to remind her that my mother has cancer, that all of this happened more or less accidentally, and that I would gladly turn back the clock and give the entire situation some more thought if it were possible.

"You are both pathetic," she snarls.

"I know I am," I offer. "I've always been pathetic." I attempt to laugh.

But answering her was a mistake, because now she looks like she might grab one of our groovy druggist statues and bash my head in with it. Then, in a flash, she looks almost embarrassed to be speaking to me and she practically runs out the door. On her feet are those brown pumps she was wearing when I was under their bed. Through the window behind my register, I watch her get into the yellow Trans Am, light one of her Newports, and peel out of the parking lot.

It takes me about half an hour to recover. Finally, the light on the phone goes off and I walk back to find Emory. He's got a freshly made vodka and V8.

"Hey there, Smiley," he says. "You look like you saw a goddamned ghost."

"Want me to vacuum?" I ask. Suddenly I have the urge to clean.

"You want to vacuum?" he asks me. "Somebody call the Pope. This is a goddamned miracle."

He bolts into the office and drags out the big old-fashioned vacuum cleaner with a red bag and a silver bottom.

"Don't you challenge those paper clips again," he says.

He says this because the last time I vacuumed I apparently sucked up about fifty paper clips and broke the machine.

"Old Smiley here," he says to Dale, "she won't pick up those paper clips, she challenges them." He laughs.

I plug in the vacuum and start rolling it up and down the aisles. The carpet looks cleaner where I've rolled over it, and I experience a weird sense of accomplishment, something I don't have very often. I leave each aisle cleaner than I found it. The noise is somewhat soothing as it drowns out the light FM station that plays Kenny Rogers and Christopher Cross songs over and over again. When I see a paper clip on the rug, I try to vacuum around it. The red bag puffs out as the powerful machine sucks up the dirt. I want to push that vacuum forever, but there are only six aisles and the gift section. Finally, Emory pulls the plug on me.

"Want to dust?" he asks as I wheel the vacuum back toward the office.

"Not really," I say.

Emory laughs because he thinks it is funny that I won't even do my usual fake dusting unless I'm in the right mood. I hate dusting. If there were a machine involved, I might like it, but I don't like having to move things around.

The Happy Family Chinese Restaurant

"HAVE YOU LOST ANY WEIGHT YET?" I ask.

"Can't you tell?" Mr. Howland sucks in his stomach. In addition to the burger-and-tomato diet, he had been running every day. Summer's almost here, and he wants to get in shape. He stopped running because some kids in a car threw a cupful of ice out their window at him. Believe it or not, the shards of ice left little cuts across his forehead.

We are riding in Mr. Howland's car. Even though we've been messing around for over two months now, this is our first night on the town. He is taking me out for dinner. He even called me from his own house to invite me; normally these days, I'd be at therapy on a Wednesday afternoon, but Dr. Chester rescheduled. I was glad I decided to answer the phone. Mr. Howland picked a restaurant way out on Route 88, so far out that the chances of either one of us knowing anyone are very slim. It is still daylight when we pull into the parking lot; the red neon Happy Family sign is beginning to glow in the darkening sky. Neon chopsticks blink on and off.

What I feel as we go through the door is terror. It isn't quite as bad as the terror I felt under the Howlands' bed, or in the car driving to the hospital with my father, but it is terror nonetheless. I am hallucinating that I see Patty and her mother and Mrs. Howland and even my mother sitting in a booth together over by the fish tank. But the reality is that the place is practically empty. We sit down across from the tank, which contains two or three skinny, sick-looking lobsters. Mr. Howland orders beef with broccoli, and I order wonton soup. My goal has changed from enjoying a night out with Mr. Howland to eating as fast as possible and getting the hell out of here.

"Guess what?" Mr. Howland says. He's hogging the crunchy noodles and duck sauce, but I don't say anything.

"What?"

"Guess who is going to New York City?"

"Who?"

"We are." He smiles very broadly.

"How are we going to do that?" I ask.

"A class trip," he says. "We're going to see art galleries in SoHo."

"Our class?"

"Yes, our class and Ron's painting class."

"When are we going?"

"Two weeks," he answers. "So don't forget your permission slip."

"What about Patty?" I ask. "Does this mean Patty is going?"

Ever since the night at her house, I have developed a terrible fear of Patty. She won't talk to me or look at me anymore, and I'm constantly worried that she is going to spill the beans. In addition, since that night, the phone at my house keeps ringing, but when I pick up, no one is on the line. I suspect someone is trying to drive me insane so that I'll confess.

"Don't worry about Patty," Mr. Howland says. "I'll turn on the old Howland charm for both her and Old Leather Head."

Old Leather Head is Mr. Howland's name for Patty's mother.

"They'll melt like butter."

After we finish eating, Mr. Howland and I open our fortune cookies at the same time. I get a pretty good fortune. It says, "You will get everything you desire and more." Mr. Howland looks kind of pissed about his. He hands it to me and I read, "Be careful of . . ." The rest of the words are blurry.

"Cheap Chinese ink," Mr. Howland says.

I eat both cookies. Mr. Howland's fortune does unsettle me because I've never seen a fortune before that you couldn't read.

When we leave the restaurant, it is pouring; giant rain-drops pound us and we are both drenched when we get into the car.

"Guess what?" I say.

"What?"

"Your wife came into the pharmacy."

"She did what?" he asks, his voice sharp.

Rain is running down the windshield in sheets.

"She asked me how I liked her husband." I laugh because telling Mr. Howland about it makes it seem less scary.

"Do you think she knows?" I ask him. The truth is I've been pretty worried since her visit.

"I don't care *what* she knows," he says. He says it quietly, emphasizing each word, but his face is red and he seems angry.

"I care," I say. "I don't want to get in trouble."

I realize now that I should have kept this information to myself because Mr. Howland looks even more upset.

"Why are you laughing about this?" He raises his voice. "Why are you even here?"

Mr. Howland is yelling now. His face is very red, so red it looks like the little cuts could break open.

"Do you give a shit about even one thing?" he asks.

"I guess I don't," I answer.

Mr. Howland punches the ceiling of the car three times. He punches it hard, as hard as he can. His fist leaves knuckle-shaped dents. If it had been my face getting punched, my head would be splattered against the passenger side window. This is a side of Mr. Howland I haven't seen before.

"Let's go," he says. He is barely able to shift gears with his right hand.

He peels out of the parking lot. We go down Route 88 faster than I've ever gone down Route 88 before.

My mind turns to the Dracula Principle. At this point it seems to me that we have lost our cloak of secrecy. Patty knows and Barbie knows and other people seem to suspect. Even Mrs. Howland knows something. The question is, Did the Dracula Principle work for Dracula, or was it simply that no one cared until it was too late? At what point did people know that Dracula was a vampire? Most important, at what point did they decide to drive that stake through his heart? Not that psychiatrists are necessarily experts on vampires, but it might be worthwhile to ask Dr. Chester a few questions during my session tomorrow.

By the time we get to the parking lot where I've left my car, Mr. Howland has calmed down quite a bit.

"I'm sorry," he says. "It just seems sometimes like this is all a big joke to you." Rather than say anything, I kiss his sore-looking fist.

Head Shrinking

It's THURSDAY, not my normal therapy day, but as I said, Dr. Chester needed to change my appointment. As usual, he is sitting behind his big desk looking bored. It is now my seventh therapy session, and it's becoming obvious to both of us I won't talk about the stuff that interests him, like my brother, my mother, my sexual fantasies, or anything else that might give him some clue about what I'm really like. In fact, whenever he brings up sex I get insanely embarrassed for both of us.

"What do you know about Dracula?" I ask.

"The vampire?"

I want to say, What other Dracula is there? But I'd rather not start off on the wrong foot again.

At our last session, I sat there for thirty minutes without saying a word. My strategy was to see if he would talk, and he didn't. I sat there waiting and waiting, examining the wooden voodoo statues and reading the framed certificates on the wall. After thirty minutes I started joking around about the statues, and then he got somewhat mad.

"Sometimes we use the therapy situation to play games that work in other areas of our lives," he told me.

"Is that right?" I answered.

"Yes," he said.

At that moment I hated his guts, and I got up and left. I walked out the door and drove away. I really didn't think I'd ever go back, but here I am. What he said bugged me, and I don't want him to think he won.

"Was there a real Count Dracula?" I ask.

"I believe it is a legend. Why are you interested in Dracula?"

"I don't know." I pause. "I've been wondering how he got people to trust him. I remember hearing somewhere that vampires can't come into your house unless you invite them in. So, people must have invited Count Dracula into their houses. That means he must have been charming or something." At that moment, the image of Mr. Howland standing outside the picture window at Patty's house pops into my head.

"That is part of the legend," Dr. Chester says. "And in the movies, Dracula usually is a very charming character."

"But then he sucks your blood?"

"Yes, then he sucks your blood."

"And you become undead?"

"Yes," he says, "you become a zombie that, I believe, needs to drink blood to survive."

"I don't drrrink wine," I say in a Transylvanian accent, because Mr. Howland says that sometimes when he is goofing around with me, pretending to give me hickeys and whatnot while we are drinking blackberry brandy.

"Do you know someone who reminds you of Dracula?" Dr. Chester asks.

I am beginning to catch on to some principles of psychiatry, and I realize that it will probably make his day if I say my mother or my father or even him, so I pretend to think hard about the question. Naturally, I haven't told him one thing about Mr. Howland.

"Maybe you," I say, playing along.

I can see him getting all hot and interested.

"How do I remind you of Dracula?"

"Because you don't drrrink wine."

He looks at me carefully.

"And because you're going to suck my blluud," I say.

"Is that how this feels to you," he asks, "like I want to suck your blood?"

"Yes, that is how it feels." I speak more seriously, without the accent. "You want to know everything about me so you can turn me into a zombie."

"Why would I want to turn you into a zombie?" he asks.

"So you can control me."

"What would I make you do?"

"I don't know. Visit my mother."

He waits a few seconds.

"Do you want someone to make you visit your mother?" he asks. "Would that make it easier?"

"You can't force me to do that," I say.

"Do you wish I could?" he asks. "Do you wish I had that much power?"

I'm trying to figure out where he is going with this, but I feel that I am a step or two behind him.

"You think I'm wrong, don't you?" I ask. "You think it is pretty lousy of me to stay away."

"Do I?" he responds.

"Do you?"

"I'm not here to make those kinds of judgments," he says.

I want to explain the feeling I have that I am somehow behind everything, the cause of my mother's sickness and of every other crappy thing that happens.

"I believe in Dracula," I tell him. "I believe in many kinds of monsters."

I feel the presence of the monster from my childhood nightmare, and then I tell him about it, about the being that drained the life out of me night after night. After listening to the entire dream and making me repeat key points, Dr. Chester reminds me that the monster always failed. He reminds me that I was stronger than the monster was, at least in the dream, and that it was the monster that needed *me* in order to survive, not the other way around.

By the time we finish, I am so exhausted I can barely drive without falling asleep at the wheel of my car.

Kippy

AT HOME, KIPPY IS THERE. She's back from the veterinarian's office, and naturally, she is sitting in the gold chair waiting for my mother. My father has left for the hospital, so I go to the kitchen to see if he left me any food. There is cold pizza in the refrigerator and a can of Mighty Dog on the counter. I decide to try to make a Mighty Dog special burger for Kippy. After watching Mr. Howland make about five hundred hamburgers, I feel qualified. I pack the dog food into a hamburger shape and put it in a frying pan and throw some cheese on top. Kippy must smell it, because I see her small gray shape coming into the room, sniffing the air like something familiar is happening for a change. After the cheese melts, I put the little burger on a human plate and blow on it until it cools down. Kippy is standing there at my feet waiting for her burger. When it hits the floor, she eats the entire thing right away, and then she even follows me to the bottom of the stairs. For a minute I think she's going to come up to the second floor with me, but she licks her chops and goes back to the gold chair to wait.

Going to the Moon

IT'S FUNNY, but on Friday night I decide to call Barbie and try to do something with people my own age. Mr. Howland can't get out of the house, and I don't feel like sitting around alone while my father is in the city. Barbie is actually psyched to hear from me—she tells me to meet her at her house at around eight o'clock because everyone is going to the Moon, a place I've never been before.

When I get to Barbie's house, we go into her bedroom because she needs to use the curling iron on her hair. Her room is the same from when we were little kids except for the fact that now her vanity has become something like what a movie star might use to get herself ready for a scene. Barbie really is a terrific-looking girl. It was weird, because until ninth grade no one even noticed her, but then her breasts doubled in size and she grew her hair long and the best-looking boys couldn't stop talking about her. She's had a boyfriend each year since then. I flip through our old junior high yearbook looking at the people whose faces we put x's through and the things we wrote next to pictures of people we hated.

"So how's your boyfriend?" she asks as she uses the curling iron to flip back the front of her strawberry blond hair. "Or should I say your man friend?"

"His wife came into the pharmacy," I tell her.

"You're shitting me," she says. She puts down the curling iron and stares at me.

"No, really," I say. "She bought some cigarettes."

"Does she know? Is that why she came in?"

"I don't know," I say. "I think she does."

I'm sitting at the end of Barbie's bed, on the soft worn-out quilt that she has always had. Grand Funk Railroad is playing softly in the background.

"Did she say anything?" Barbie asks.

"Yeah, she said some stuff about her husband, and then she gave me a weird look."

"What kind of look?"

"Like maybe she hates my freaking guts," I say. We both start laughing, but I can tell by the way Barbie's looking at me that she's worried.

I keep flipping through the yearbook until I see a familiar, round face.

"Remember Michael Parks?" I say.

"You mean that fat kid in the slow class?"

"Remember he always used to say that he was going to take you out in his five-door Cadillac?"

"What did we write?" she asks.

"It's mean," I say.

She sits down next to me on the bed, and we look at the picture of Michael Parks and what is written in black marker in a bubble over his head: "I am a moron." But we laugh anyway.

I flip through some more until I find Tyrone Love. The print quality of the book is so poor that you can hardly see his face. At least we didn't write anything mean over his picture.

"Are you scared?" Barbie asks as she pulls a soft baby-blue cowl-neck sweater over her head.

"Not really," I say. "I don't know what to be scared of."

"Is Patty still pissed at you?" she asks.

"I think so. What's she doing tonight?"

"She's coming over with Cathy and Gail."

"Balls," I say, an expression I've stolen from Mr. Howland.

"She was a crazy woman that night," Barbie says. "I thought she was going to crash right through the door Frankenstein-style."

We both start laughing again. Patty was like a bull that night.

"Are you afraid of her?" I ask Barbie. "Because I am."

"You should be afraid of her. She practically broke my arm holding me back. I was going to warn you, but I couldn't let on that I knew anything."

"Thanks for trying," I say.

"For someone so skinny, she's really strong," Barbie says.

"Are you still with Billy?"

"Yeah, we had broken up, but he called yesterday and we're back together."

We hear Gail and Patty and Cathy come in the front door, and we get up and give each other a look that says, Oh well, and we walk out.

We take Barbie's mother's station wagon, also known as "the magic bus," out to the Moon. I ride shotgun with Barbie, and Patty rides in the back. We haven't said anything to each other, but there is definite tension in the air. I have a vague, sick feeling in my stomach, but I don't think I'm going to puke or anything. Cathy has this sad, thin-looking joint that she stole from her brother's wallet, so Barbie pops in the lighter and we wait to smoke it up.

Cathy has a glass eye, and her favorite thing to do is to hang out and play gin rummy with her family in their big old RV. She always has pot, and it's consistently tragic weed. But we'll smoke it even if it's harsh because Gail forgot her fake ID. Mr. Howland said he was going to make me a fake license on a silk screen so that I can go into bars with him, but he hasn't done it yet. It's kind of clear that no one is used to me being around. Some of the kids still treat me like a freak because I won a spelling bee in front of the whole school back in eighth grade. That spelling bee got me labeled as a loser. Actually, ever since fourth grade I've gotten weird looks on account of the fact that I used to have a larger than normal vocabulary. Believe me, having a larger than normal vocabulary at my school isn't too tricky. These days, I mostly successfully hide any intelligence I have, but every now and then a big, awkward-sounding word pops out at the wrong moment.

The truth is that I used to be smart. I learned to read before I went to school, and they even tested me to see if I was a genius or something. I used to sit in first grade thinking that the kids in my class were pretending to be stupid. They couldn't even read a Dick and Jane book. It was horrible to listen to them sounding out a word like "Spot." I was the smartest kid back then. But between my trying to use small words and school getting tougher, I honestly think I've gotten dumber every year of my life. In fact, at last check, I was barely making a C in Geometry. Still, it is pretty nuts how even one multisyllable word thrown in at the wrong moment can destroy your social life. Fortunately, for whatever reasons, I am allowed to hang around with the cool people at school when I am so inclined.

As I said, I've never been to the Moon before because it is a relatively new place for people to hang out and I've been MIA for the past couple months because of Mr. Howland. We are driving in the same direction as the secret spot, and it's getting weird when finally we go a different direction altogether. Cathy lights up her skinny joint and passes it around.

"What is this crap?" Patty asks, coughing.

"My brother grew it in his bedroom," Cathy says.

The Moon, it turns out, is a big crater in the ground in the middle of a gravel pit. Because of the lack of trees or anything green whatsoever, I guess it does somewhat resemble the moon. There is a pool of shiny water near the crater, the kind of water that would probably transform you into a radioactive mutant if you drank it or even put your foot in it. New Jersey is loaded with these kinds of pools.

There are kids standing around drinking beers, while others are sitting in the sand, and people run up when the magic bus arrives to say hello. A few kids are happy to see me, and I'm glad to be here. Someone hands me a beer, and I wander about as far away from Patty as I can get. People tend to let me enter into groups because I don't really say much and I can look sort of tough and detached when necessary. So I stand on the edge of a group of boys I've gone to school with since first grade. One of the boys was my first boyfriend, but when he tried to put his hand inside my shirt on the Sky Ride at Great Adventure, I broke up with him. Now that seems prudy because I've done so much more than that. With Mr. Howland, sex has never felt awkward, probably because he knows what to do.

To be honest, the party is pretty boring. The same stuff happens on the Moon that happens back on Earth. Barbie gets into an argument with Billy because he's jealous, Denise Degrasso gets drunk and starts crying. Tara Herlan's boyfriend gets drunk and "accidentally" pees on her. It's difficult not to wish I was out in the secret spot with Mr. Howland. The only interesting thing is that there is a group of boys from another school standing on the other shore of the mutant pool. They look a bit less raggedy than the kids from my school. In fact, there is a very tall boy with dark hair who is looking at me like he wants to say hi. Being the antisocial person I am, I turn my back on him and pretend to be interested in the people I'm with.

By the time we leave, our shoes are caked with sandy mud and the magic bus is getting incredibly dirty. Billy is going to drive home with us, so I have to sit in the way back. Patty climbs in there with me, and I can see that she's got something she wants to say.

"You're going to get caught, you know," she says.

I don't say anything. I sit there staring forward.

"You can't keep it up," she says. "It isn't fair to Melinda."

For a moment, I wonder if it could be Patty herself calling my house and hanging up when I answer.

"I know," I say.

"Are you going to stop seeing him?" she asks.

"Yeah," I say.

"I don't want my mother to find out, because she'll kill me for knowing and she'll call both your mother and his wife," she says. "My mother is already worried about you."

"What's she worried about?"

"You're acting like a freak around everyone."

I close my eyes. Patty seems satisfied with the warning she's given, and I lean back and listen to Styx singing "Come Sail Away" from the radio and the voices of everyone saying things at once. Billy has his arm around Barbie in the front seat, and it makes me feel sorry for myself because my own boyfriend could never go to the Moon on a Friday night and even if he could, he probably wouldn't want to.

Bracelets

I'VE NOTICED THAT TEACHERS talk about what interests *them*, not what interests us. With Mr. Sikorsky, it's the Depression. With Mr. Wallace, it is wrestling, Oliver Cromwell, and the Fox. Mr. Aniello's obsession is Vietnam. He spent the entire first half of the period today talking about Vietnam, explaining to us that seeing people get shot on television is nothing like seeing them get shot in person. He tried to describe the way blood spurts out of a real gunshot wound as he ran across the room pretending to have been shot in the leg. During the second half of class, we listened to a presentation by a girl I don't know very well. She'd researched the Buddhist monks who set themselves on fire to protest the war in Vietnam. She even had a photograph of a peaceful-looking monk in orange robes engulfed in flames. This girl's father was killed in Vietnam. In junior high a couple of boys got suspended for making fun of her for wearing his dog tags to school.

Though Mr. Aniello's Sociology class can be enlightening at times, it is difficult to admire him because he could be the most uncool teacher in the entire school. Still, as uncool as he is, he is difficult to put into a category. He's not a hippie because he embraces the disco culture in a pretty big way. And he doesn't dress like a hippie. He wears polyester shirts featuring geometric patterns and colorful scenes. He calls the ugliest one, a shirt with a picture of a guy riding a giant unicycle, his Horatio Alger shirt. He even wears platform shoes. The saddest and most pathetic part is that he once told us he keeps his best clothes at home in his closet and only wears them when he goes out dancing. The thought of him putting on his best clothes and going out dancing makes me feel incredibly depressed. The kids call him Disco Dick and Tony Manero behind his back.

At lunch I tell Mr. Howland about Mr. Aniello's class and about how he tries to make us care about Vietnam. Both of us have pretty much forgotten about the trip to the Chinese restaurant.

"I was in Vietnam," Mr. Howland says. "Look at this."

He lifts up the leg of his pants and reveals a big ugly scar I've never noticed before.

"I got shot at Hamburger Hill," he says.

"You were in Vietnam?" I ask. For a second I am surprised. The thought of Mr. Howland being in a war is pretty exciting.

"Ha!" he practically shouts. "Gotcha! Had you going there for a second, didn't I? That's a scar where I had a mole removed."

"Yuck," I say. I probably should have known that Mr. Howland wouldn't have been in Vietnam and that his reference to hamburgers was an obvious clue.

"How come you didn't have to go?" I ask.

"I went to graduate school and I got married," he says. "Do you think I'm crazy enough to go get killed in some jungle in Vietnam?"

I do believe that being a complete weirdo like Mr. Aniello might be better than being some sort of coward. But I'll tell you, these days it has become pretty much impossible to tell who is a coward and who isn't. My father hates hippies and anyone who went to Canada instead of going to Vietnam. He drove us through Haight-Ashbury on a family vacation in 1971, and he told me that hippies lived in holes in the ground like rats. That is not an easy image to get out of your head. On the other hand, as I've already mentioned, every single person I know of who was in Vietnam isn't doing that well. The older brother of the kid who used to live next door to me supposedly died "cleaning his gun." After he came back from the war, he didn't get a job and almost never left the house. Every now and then he walked around the neighborhood, always wearing a green army jacket. My guess is he wasn't cleaning anything; he put that gun in his mouth and pulled the trigger.

Rather than talk any more about Vietnam, I switch to telling Mr. Howland about my trip to the Moon. I watch his face, and it's easy to see that he is not listening. He doesn't take too much of an interest in my life outside of him; he makes it seem like high school is this time of life you won't even remember, so there's no point in talking about anything that happens. He gets bored hearing about Barbie's problems with Billy or how Denise got drunk at a party, topics that I admit are not exactly scintillating subjects for conversation. We do better if we stick to his favorite topics. I don't necessarily love hearing about how annoying his wife is and how much this school stinks, but Mr. Howland is a knowledgeable person, and he will tell me gossip about teachers.

I'm sitting at the table with him, but he hasn't made a hamburger for a few days because he is sick of washing the electric hot plate. Gary Ivers went out and got him a sub and a Coke that he is sharing with me; I don't say anything about the diet because I was getting tired of watching him eat meat and tomatoes every day. About halfway through lunch, he gives me a present wrapped up in white paper. It is probably because he is an artist, but he always makes things look nice—the white paper is tied with a red ribbon and my name is written on the package. It says "To my love, Edna."

Inside the package is a silver bracelet that looks exactly like the one he wears on his left wrist. It's more petite, though, a ladies-size bracelet. His is more like a silver cuff. Both of them are a very simple design, in accordance with Mr. Howland's aesthetic of simplicity and functionality, yet they share a similar pattern.

"Won't people notice?" I ask.

"I don't give a good god damn," he says.

I slide the bracelet onto my wrist, and it fits perfectly. It's a nice bracelet.

"It looks like we are in the same club," I say.

"We are," Mr. Howland says.

The pervert club, I think to myself, but I don't say it because I can see that Mr. Howland is taking this whole thing seriously. With this piece of matching jewelry, he is claiming me. It feels good and bad at the same time, because part of me really wants to be claimed and the other part of me is quite frightened of what is going to happen. But if you could see how happy it makes him to see me wearing it, you would understand why I love him so much. He is talented in so many different ways. He can draw, paint, and make a perfect bracelet. He can shift gears without using the clutch and fix the brake pads on his own car. He made me like *folk* music. Mr. Howland sees beauty in things that other people take for granted. He even sees beauty in me.

"What if Patty notices it?" I ask.

"I'm not worried about Patty," he insists.

I am, though. Patty is a smart girl. She is angry and worried at the same time. Mr. Howland seems not to notice that the force of Patty's anger and her mother's anger and their negative judgment is just as strong as, if not stronger than, the Dracula Principle. Mr. Howland might even be losing touch with reality. He seems to be forgetting about his wife and my father and everyone else in the world who is going to want to have a say about this.

"Stop worrying," he says.

Lately, Mr. Howland has been making pottery again. He gave us an assignment to work on independently, a research project on an artist we admire, and told us not to bug him unless absolutely necessary. Because no teacher or principal oversees what goes on in any given classroom, Mr. Howland is free to do as he pleases. He sits at the potter's wheel shaping the same lump of clay into various forms, always simple and functional. One day he'll make a vase, the next a bowl. Today he's making a plate. While he works, he listens to almost nothing but old Rod Stewart and the Rolling Stones. His favorite songs are "You Wear It Well" and "Lost Paraguayos" by Rod Stewart and "Beast of Burden" by the Stones, songs he sometimes plays over and over again. The strange part is that he is never satisfied with the finished product and ends up starting over. Rather than a bracelet, I wish Mr. Howland would give me one of those beautiful tall vases before he destroys it. If I could make even one symmetrical piece of pottery, I'd save it forever. Today as he works, he's blasting Dylan's *Highway 61 Revisited*, something new for a change. We sit at the desks with our art books pretending that it is normal for the teacher to be sitting at the wheel ignoring us while listening to "Ballad of a Thin Man" loud enough for the kids in the next room to hear.

Dr. Chester's Office

It is Wednesday afternoon and I am back in Dr. Chester's waiting room. Outside it is drizzling. For the first time since I started coming here, I see the person who had the appointment before mine. From the window I can see that he's walking out the secret exit and heading to his car. He begins to jog because of the rain. He's dressed in a business suit, and he drives a small blue sedan. I feel myself getting very interested to know why a grown man would be going in the middle of the afternoon to talk to Dr. Chester. Shouldn't a grown man be able to solve his own problems? It can't be that his mother is making him come here. As I'm wondering about this, the door opens and Dr. Chester is standing there. I follow him in without making my usual stupid face.

"So, how are you?" he asks as I sit down.

"You talked first," I say.

He looks like he surprised himself. "I suppose I did," he says.

I offer up the generic rundown of recent events—the return of Kippy from the vet's office, my triumphant Mighty Dog cooking experience, and a few made-up concerns about school. He's nodding his head as usual.

"Is it weird to have an invisible friend?" I ask him.

"Do you have one?" he asks. He smiles.

"No," I say, "I don't have one now, but I did. His name was Sucan, and he was half-human and half-chipmunk. I used to play Monopoly with him and cheat."

"That doesn't seem right," Dr. Chester says. "Even if he was invisible."

I'm glad Dr. Chester isn't treating me like a freak for having Sucan. Because Sucan was actually a very good friend of mine. He was always willing to play whatever game I wanted to play.

"What happened to him?"

"I don't know," I answer. "I think I made a few human friends and he stopped showing up. He was real for a while. There was a time with Sucan when I wasn't pretending. But then, at a certain point, I knew I was making him up."

It occurs to me that this emotional progression from fantasy to reality might be true of relationships with human beings as well.

"It sounds like he helped you with some loneliness," Dr. Chester says.

"Hey," I say, finally ready to bring up my brother again. "I asked my father about Tommy."

"Good for you," he says. "That must have been difficult."

"Turns out he wasn't murdered." I'm telling Dr. Chester this very cheerfully, like I just found out the ending of a TV show that I missed.

"Did you find out what did happen?" he asks.

"He drowned," I say. "After all that, it turns out that he drowned. That psychiatrist was with him."

Dr. Chester looks sad, not sorry for me, he just looks sad that my brother died. Dr. Chester seems to me to be the kind of guy who probably wouldn't have let someone like Tommy out of his sight. I bet he would have been more careful with him.

"Was it hard for you to ask about Tommy?" he asks.

Hearing Dr. Chester say Tommy's name makes him seem more real to me, real in a way that he hasn't felt before. It's hard to stay cheerful, because Dr. Chester seems to be changing the tone.

"To be honest," I tell him, "I was kind of relieved."

"How so?"

"Because I asked my father and I expected him to yell at

me or something, to tell me to mind my own business, but he wasn't like that."

"What was he like?"

"He acted like he thought it was a perfectly normal thing to ask. He actually seemed kind of glad to tell me."

"Do you have any ideas about why it was such a relief to find out how Tommy died?" he asks.

I glance around again, and I think about Mr. Howland getting hit in the face with a cupful of ice and I think about Mrs. Howland's visit to the pharmacy and about the man walking to his car who had been sitting in the seat right before me. I am staring at a painting behind Dr. Chester's head. It is a painting of a white house in a field of golden wheat. I try to get a clear picture of Sucan in my mind, but I can't. Outside, it is still drizzling.

"Maybe," I say.

He waits. I'm biting my thumbnail. I'm remembering how Barbie asked me so bluntly about Tommy. I tried to cover up how stunned I was. But I believed her. I really believed it was possible that someone murdered him.

"I thought someone killed him," I say. "That could be why I never asked anyone about it."

"Why would someone kill him?" he asks.

"I'm still not sure," I say.

"Why aren't you sure?"

"Because what I'm saying is that I honestly thought it was true."

I keep looking at that painting, but I'm not seeing much.

"Do you feel relief because he wasn't murdered, or are you relieved about something else?" Dr. Chester asks.

"What else would I be relieved about?"

"Well," he says, "maybe you have always been glad that you didn't have to deal with this brother who had so many problems."

"Are you saying it happened because of me?"

"Is that what you think?" he asks.

"No," I say. "It was my parents."

"So you think it was your parents who did it?"

"They may have decided to do it after I was born," I say. "So I could be normal."

"How would that work?" he asks.

"How would I know?" I snap back.

I wait for a while because some strange ideas are coming to me; thoughts are rushing into my mind.

"Maybe they did it so I wouldn't have to have an autistic brother."

"You're saying they would have done it to make your life more normal?"

I think about Tyrone Love and how the kids in school make fun of him because he gets angry for no reason and hits himself in the face. Think about this: if winning a stupid spelling bee can make people shun you, what would it mean to have a brother who couldn't talk?

"I think so," I say. "I think it would have been worse for me if he were here. I would have been a complete outcast. They needed to save me."

"But it doesn't seem like his death has made things easier for your parents," he says. "Why would they do something that caused so much heartache?"

I think he may be referring to the fact that I've told him about how my parents both seem pretty sad a lot of the time.

"If I'd turned out better, it might have been worth it."

"How?" he asks.

"I wish at least I could have been more normal for them."

"You mean for your parents?"

"I wish I wasn't always so scared of everything."

"You had reasons to be afraid," he says. "There were things you didn't understand that scared you."

"I've messed up everything," I say. "I've made some pretty big messes."

I think about what I said to my mother the night she found out she had cancer, how I yelled at her that by not letting me go to that stupid party she was trying to turn me into a freak like she did to my brother.

"I think he died because of me," I say.

"You mean your brother?" Dr. Chester asks.

"Yes."

"How could it have been?" he says. "Your father told you it was an accident."

"But what if it was still somehow because of me?"

"Tell me, how could it have been because of you? Now you know what really happened," he says. "You thought you had the answer figured out, but you were wrong. Maybe not everything happens because of you."

"My mother got sick because of me, because we were fighting."

"Now you want the power to cause cancer? What else can you do?"

We sit there without talking for a minute or two, me thinking about how you can find out there are things in your mind that you didn't know were there. Dr. Chester looks tired. But he looks tired in the way a person who just won a race or a boxing match looks tired. He offers me a tissue, and it is funny because until that moment I didn't even know I was crying. If you'd asked me, I would have told you that I was smiling.

"Maybe I did something wrong?" I suggest.

"Our time is up," he says.

"Just like that?" I ask.

"We can talk more next week," he says.

I walk out to my car through the same door as the man before me. The rain has stopped, but the sky is still very cloudy and threatening. I feel strangely similar to the way I did after my first trip to the secret spot with Mr. Howland. This time, however, I don't feel any older or smarter. I feel sad. I have discovered yet another new place inside me. This place I've discovered is not a new continent. It is a black hole, and I don't know how to fill it up.

Another Telephone Call

IT IS THURSDAY NIGHT and I am at home alone because my father is at the hospital in New York as usual. I feed Kippy and am trying to write an essay on Macbeth's tragic flaw when the phone rings. I pick it up on the second ring and say hello. I am about ready to put down the receiver thinking that it is the anonymous hang-up person again when I hear a voice.

"Is your mother home?" a woman says.

"No," I reply.

"Will she be back soon?" she asks.

"I don't know," I say.

We are both silent for a second.

"Would you like to leave a message?" I ask.

"No," she says, "I'll call back."

"Why don't you leave my mother out of this?" I say.

She hangs up. I could not say with 100 percent certainty, but the voice on the other end sounded like Mr. Howland's wife. I feel myself getting angry about recent events, about Mrs. Howland and her mysterious visit to the pharmacy and Mr. Howland and his not teaching anymore. I'm angry at my mother for leaving me home alone. I wish my father were here. I wish I could hear the sound of Marv Albert's voice or the sound of machine-gun fire or any other television show to drown out the silence after that phone call.

This Isn't Philadelphia

ON SATURDAY MORNING the phone rings pretty early, and I'm contemplating not answering because of the recent string of mysterious phone calls, but I'm glad I do answer because it is Mr. Howland himself calling.

"Good morning," he says.

This is only the second time we've spoken on the phone.

"Can you meet me in the back of the parking lot at school by the industrial arts building in about an hour?" he asks.

"Sure," I say.

"Wear something nice," he says. "Something not ripped."

My father is not home, and I'm not clear where he is. He could be at work or he could be on his way to New York. Either way, I am free to do as I please.

I wear jeans that are neither ripped nor patched and a white sweater that my mother bought me for going out to dinner and such. I have to admit, this sweater does look nice on me, but as I usually prefer T-shirts or my father's old shirts, I don't feel entirely comfortable. When I'm uncomfortable, I sweat a lot, and I hope I don't wreck this nice sweater.

I drive over to the high school with the windows down because it is a beautiful sunny day. My heart lifts up when I see Mr. Howland's car already sitting by itself in the empty parking lot. I pull up next to him, but as I'm getting out of the car he gets out instead.

"Can we take your car?" he asks. "I'm pretending to be working today."

"Okay," I say.

"I'll drive," he tells me.

It is funny because I've never been a passenger in my car before. I'm not even sure if my car would like to be driven by someone else. Mr. Howland brings a fake-leather box containing cassette tapes with him. He's wearing black jeans and a white shirt.

Mr. Howland looks too big for the Triumph—it is a sports car with only two seats, and his head practically touches the ceiling.

"Can you tell me where we are going now?" I ask him.

"South Jersey," he says.

"What for?"

"We're going to have lunch with a friend of mine who lives near Philadelphia."

My stomach seizes up, and the sweat starts dripping down my sides. At the same time, it is exciting to be meeting a friend of Mr. Howland's. He knows my friends, but I've never met any of his. I think about Goose Pond. Mr. Howland must have his own Goose Ponds, places that are important to him that I've never been. This may even explain why he took me to his house that day. He's trying to show me things about himself. So even though none of our other excursions have turned out particularly well, I decide to go to South Jersey with him.

As we drive, we listen to *Led Zeppelin II*, one of Mr. Howland's all-time favorite albums. He particularly likes "Whole Lotta Love," a song he told me that he plays when he and his wife have a fight. He blasts it and she hates it. Having seen the speakers of their stereo, I can imagine that it must get pretty loud. Mostly we joke around as we drive, probably to dispel the nervousness of going out into public again.

"I'm surprised you have friends," I say.

"Very funny."

"Who is this we're meeting?"

"Tim and I went to graduate school together in New York," Mr. Howland says.

Mr. Howland being in graduate school in New York is hard to imagine. Sometimes it is easy to forget that Mr. Howland has lived other places and done things other than cook hamburgers, make sculptures, and take me to the secret spot.

"Will we be near the Pine Barrens?" I ask.

"Somewhat," he says.

"I've always wanted to see the Jersey Devil," I say.

"You're looking at him," Mr. Howland says, and laughs.

After about an hour of driving, we finally get to our destination. Mr. Howland has a happy expression on his face. The houses in this town are nicely kept up, mostly white with lots of flowers. It looks like the kind of town you might go to on vacation but not actually live in. We pull into a parking lot behind a three-story office building.

"Tim wanted us to meet him at his loft," Mr. Howland tells me.

"What's a loft?" I ask. Once again, the sweat is soaking my armpits.

"It's his studio," Mr. Howland answers.

We leave my car in the parking lot and walk up two flights of stairs. We come out into a wide hallway, and Mr. Howland leads me through a door. We enter a room filled with canvases and easels and paints. Across the room I see a man who appears to be older than Mr. Howland. This man has gray hair.

"Tim," Mr. Howland says as the gray-haired man walks toward us. "I want you to meet Edna." Mr. Howland is smiling. He looks proud of me.

"Hi, Edna," Tim says.

The expression on Tim's face is hard to read. He seems uncomfortable. I hold my arms down by my sides to hide the wetness.

Mr. Howland is happier than I have seen him in a while. He walks around studying paintings.

"This place is great," he says. "I wish I'd never started teaching."

I am completely unable to speak, and I know trying would be a mistake. I just follow behind Mr. Howland, pretending to examine the art.

"So, Sawyer, how's Melinda?" Tim asks, and he instantly realizes this is a weird question, given the situation.

"Melinda was in grad school with us," Mr. Howland tells me. "Tim dated her first. But *he* was smart enough not to marry her."

"Maybe if you hadn't stolen her away, I would have," Tim says.

"Let's go to lunch," Mr. Howland says, ignoring Tim's comment.

Because my car is so small, we take Tim's car. Mr. Howland had talked about the Philadelphia cheesesteak sandwich that he was going to have for the entire ride to South Jersey.

"You can't get a *real* cheesesteak sandwich anywhere but Philly," he says now.

"This isn't Philadelphia," I point out. It is the first thing I have said since we arrived and the sound of my voice is alarming even to me.

"No," Tim says, "but we're close enough to get a good one."

I look at Tim and think about Mr. Howland's life. If this is Mr. Howland's Goose Pond, then I have fallen through the ice—even worse, the hole I've fallen through has solidified over my head. If my mother were here, she would tell me that I am making a terrible impression. I have lost the power to speak.

At lunch, Mr. Howland and Tim tell stories about their time in New York. They talk about bars they liked. Some of the stories include references to Melinda, but because I have become a statue, it doesn't matter what they are talking about. Tim can't ask me questions because I am in high school and that is something we aren't mentioning. He does look at my bracelet, though. He looks at it long enough to know that Mr. Howland has one exactly like it.

Finally, we go back to the studio, and I get into the passenger seat of my own car. Tim and Mr. Howland are standing about ten feet away, but I can hear them talking.

"It's the real deal," Mr. Howland is saying. "This is the first good thing to happen in a long time."

I can't fully make out Tim's response. But the look on his face and his gestures make me think he's telling Mr. Howland to stop seeing me. I start to hate Tim, but I realize it is not his fault that our trip was a failure. My face starts burning when I reflect on the fact that the only words I said the entire time we were together were "This isn't Philadelphia."

Mr. Howland gets in beside me and kisses me very softly on the cheek. He squeezes my knee.

"Let's go to Philadelphia and walk through that giant heart," I suggest.

"What are you talking about?" he asks.

"It's in the Franklin Institute, I think. I went through it a long time ago, back in middle school," I tell him. "You see the blood pumping through the veins and arteries and you can hear the thumping. Mrs. Snell had to drag me out of there."

"We have to get back," he says.

"Are you mad because I didn't talk?" I ask.

"No, because I love you no matter what you do," he says. "I really do, Edna, and I don't give a damn what anyone else thinks about it."

We are finally out on the turnpike when my car starts making a strange banging sound.

"Yikes," Mr. Howland says.

"We'll make it," I say.

We turn up the radio and ignore the intermittent clangs coming from the engine. We don't talk because I believe we are both praying that the car makes it safely back. I close my eyes and picture the blood flowing through my veins and arteries, my heart the last stop. Neither one of us says it, but it is obvious to both of us that the lunch didn't go very well. Mr. Howland looks both exhausted and relieved as he drives up next to his car.

"We made it," he says.

"Here we are," I say.

We kiss goodbye, and I climb into my car's driver's seat. Mr. Howland pulls out, but I wait a few minutes longer, waiting for my heart to stop thumping. Looking toward the school building, I think I see my Latin teacher, Ms. Clewell, popping her head out the window of her classroom on the second floor. I slide down in the seat and wait until I can remind myself that she would have no reason to be at school on a Saturday afternoon. I inch my head above the door and glance toward the window where I thought I saw her, but there is no one there.

As I leave the school parking lot, there is looseness in the steering column, but fortunately the clanging sound has stopped. The play in the wheel gives me the feeling that I have less control than I did before. I turn the opposite direction from Mr. Howland's house as I head for home.

A Day Without Mr. Howland

Mr. Howland is absent on Monday, which makes being at school feel entirely pointless to me. In Latin, I wait to see if Ms. Clewell looks at me any differently, but we go over the translations the same as any other day. At the end of class, she hands back our most recent test, and I feel gratified as I see "92%" circled in red pen at the top of my paper. But then, looking more closely, I notice a small "see me" written in black ink right next to my name. I linger as everyone packs their stuff and walk up to Ms. Clewell's desk when we are alone. She shuts the door.

"Hey," she says.

"Did you want me to see you?" I ask, pointing to the message she left.

"Oh yes," she answers.

She seems as nervous as I am, if not more so.

"How are you?" she asks. "How is everything with your mother?"

"She's all right," I reply, not getting into anything personal. But I imagine Ms. Clewell is someone who might not judge me too harshly for being afraid to see my mother.

"How about *you*?" she presses, and now I begin to suspect that it was indeed her staring at me through the window.

"Good." I point to the red "92%" as evidence.

"I saw you here on Saturday," she says. "Do you want to talk about it?"

"Me? I was *here* on Saturday?" I make a face like I'm racking my brains.

"Yes," she says. "I saw you."

We pause.

"Daphne, I think you need to talk to someone about this."

"Okay, I will do that."

"I'm concerned about you."

I don't know whether to stand there looking stupid or to blurt out the whole story, from start to finish.

"It is not what you think," I tell her. "He's been helping me."

"I'll need to talk to him," Ms. Clewell says. "I know your mother is sick, but someone needs to know about this."

"You can talk to him," I say. "That's fine."

"I'll speak to you again. He can't do this." She examines me. "You might think you know what you are doing," she says, "but I assure you, you don't. You should be going to the prom and spending your time with people your own age."

She does have a point; a senior boy asked me to prom, but Mr. Howland forbade me from going.

I bolt from her classroom, happy to know that Mr. Howland is absent. After school, I try to call his house from the pay phone by the gym, but no one answers. As luck would have it, he is absent for the next few days, and by Thursday, I figure Ms. Clewell has forgotten all about it. She doesn't know much of anything other than what she saw and suspects. At this point, she has probably fallen back under the

Dracula spell. So I just wait it out. I wait and hope that things with Mr. Howland will stay as they are.

Our Class Trip

MR. HOWLAND IS BACK FRIDAY, and our class trip will take place as scheduled. It turns out that Barbie and Cathy are in Mr. Hurly's second-period class, so they are going on the trip, too. Even Tyrone is going. Patty is quite dressed up. My gut feeling is that she still has thoughts of stealing Mr. Howland away from me. She is wearing a long black skirt and a denim hippie shirt with lace and beads sewn on the seams. When we board the bus, I wonder who I'm supposed to sit with, Mr. Howland or my friends clustered around the last row of seats. If he were my regular high school boyfriend, then I'd obviously sit with Mr. Howland. Luckily for me, Mr. Hurly sits down next to him so I can go and sit with Barbie. She is still giggling over the fact that Mr. Howland and I had sex. She's giggling, but she finally gets the importance of not giving everything away by being unable to control herself.

It is obvious that even my classmates suspect Mr. Howland and me of something; they just aren't clear what it is. There must be some truth to the Dracula Principle, because no one, not even Patty or Mrs. Howland herself, is sure what to call us or what we are doing. Ms. Clewell is the wild card. Tyrone sits by himself in the seat behind Mr. Howland and

Mr. Hurly. Sitting with Barbie makes me feel somewhat normal for a change.

The first thing Barbie notices is my new bracelet. I'm wearing it to school for the first time since Mr. Howland gave it to me. "Isn't that the same bracelet Mr. Howland has?" she whispers.

I must say that for someone who gets C's in almost every subject, Barbie is extremely observant. She holds my hand and looks at the bracelet more closely.

"It's really nice," she says.

Finally, the bus pulls out of the parking lot. It's always a strange feeling to be leaving school before the day even starts; to be rolling away feels wrong somehow. What feels wrong is leaving everyone else behind to have another regular day.

A kid named Jeff Kiley brought a boom box, so we put on some music. He wants to listen to AC/DC, but the rest of us are into something more mellow because it is so early in the morning. We settle on the Boss and lean back into our seats to listen to the music and talk. Two or three of the uncool girls are sitting up close to Mr. Howland and Mr. Hurly, trying to talk to them and get attention. Tyrone is in between; he serves as a barrier between the world of teachers and the world of kids.

"Where are we going to have lunch?" Patty asks.

None of us know. The only places I've been to eat in New York are the restaurants my family went to before Knicks games. These aren't the kinds of places you'd go to for lunch on a class trip. I did bring a pretty large sum of money with me, but I don't want to wipe out my funds on lunch.

"My mother told me about a great place in the Village called the Broome Street Bar," Patty says. I see what she is up to. She is trying to lock me into having lunch with her so that Mr. Howland and I can't escape and be by ourselves.

Cathy and Barbie look at each other like they don't care one way or the other. The struggle is between Patty and me—the struggle is always between Patty and me. My silence is a pretty good indicator that I'm not going to get caught up in anything Patty says. Up to this point, Mr. Howland has taken care of everything, and he'll probably keep taking care of everything. His handsome blond hair is visible over the seat—everyone loves him. Even Mr. Hurly loves him and probably wants to have lunch with him. I'm the lucky one. He chose me, or I chose him. Maybe we chose each other.

When we come to the part of the turnpike where it smells, Barbie pulls her shirt over her face and Cathy shuts the window and everyone on the bus screams "Gross" and "Oh, yuck." Around us are the smoking cylinders of the oil refineries and the structures made from pipes and metal poles that look like the pipes that Popeye and Olive Oyl always seem to wander out on when they are being chased by Bluto. There is something weirdly beautiful about those structures and even something about the smell that is good because it is so bad.

"I wonder if we'll see my father," Cathy says.

It seems unlikely to me because there are so many differ-ent toll lanes to go through that hitting the one where Cathy's dad works would be almost impossible. But she and Barbie are craning their heads out the window and yelling for the bus driver to get to the right. It is hard to imagine what it would be like to be a toll taker on the turnpike because you need to stand in a smelly cubicle all day making change for people. My father is a lawyer, another thing that makes me different from everyone. But I'd rather be a lawyer than a toll taker any day of the week.

The Holland Tunnel is a scary place as far as I am con-cerned. The walls are dirty, dirtier than the Lincoln Tunnel. Each time I go through I start to imagine a wall of water rush-ing toward the car as the entire structure collapses. Though it's somewhat comforting to imagine swimming on top of the wave while everyone else drowns, it doesn't seem realistic. As I look around, it's clear that once again no one else is thinking what I'm thinking, because despite the darkness and the lack of clean air and windows, everyone else is talk-ing and laughing and generally having a good time.

Kids start packing their stuff when we emerge from the tunnel, and the bus driver yells for everyone to sit down. Mr. Howland catches my eye with a look that is both knowing and somewhat panicked. We will need to take some pretty in-tense evasive action to get away from everyone, most espe-cially Patty. She already has her eye on me. It seems possible that she would even grab hold of me if she thought it could keep me away from Mr. Howland. Why she wants so badly to stop me from having fun is still not clear, but there is no doubt that she'll do anything she can to keep me from Mr. Howland.

New York City

THE BUS STOPS SOMEWHERE DOWN IN SoHo, a section of New York that I'm not really familiar with; to be honest, there aren't that many parts of the city that I am familiar with. Patty is standing right at Mr. Howland's elbow, practically hanging on to the sleeve of his jacket. I give Barbie a look that says Help me, and she pulls Patty away and starts heading down the street.

"Stay on the streets marked on your maps and check off the galleries you visit," Mr. Howland yells. "Hey," he calls loudly enough that everyone stops in their tracks, "be back here at four o'clock. Don't be late or we'll leave you here. I mean it."

As soon as Mr. Howland and I see Patty getting dragged away against her will, we pretend to be going with some other kids in the opposite direction. It looks like Tyrone Love doesn't have anyone to hang around with, and that is making me nervous; luckily, Mr. Hurly senses the problem and calls Tyrone over to his group, the pack of loser kids who rely on teachers for companionship as others would their friends.

We let the other group get about a block ahead of us, and

then we turn down the first street and are free. Now, it is just Mr. Howland and me, almost like we are on a date together and not on a stupid class trip with forty other people. It is only about eleven and the galleries aren't even open, so we walk around for a while. Mr. Howland puts his arm around me for a second, but it feels weird and he takes it away. It was a simultaneous feeling of weirdness, and we both seem relieved when it is over.

Lunch

MR. HOWLAND DECIDES that we should have lunch before we head over to the galleries. I don't care one way or the other. Mostly, I find art galleries and museums to be equally boring—they make me want to run away. Something about pictures hanging on walls makes me nervous. Maybe it would be enjoyable if it were my and Tyrone's gallery—a gallery full of lopsided pots and headless statues. To be honest, I'd rather look at oil refineries from a bus window. I really would.

The restaurant Mr. Howland picks is barely open. The busboys are setting up chairs and writing the day's menu on the board outside. I look both ways for Patty and company before we duck in. We are the first customers. Mr. Howland says he's been here before. To me, it seems like the kind of place that vampires would go to drink tall glasses of blood. Our waiter could be a vampire, or one of those guys in school that no one talks to because they wear black lipstick and look like drug addicts. But I should talk; me and Mr. Howland must make a strange pair ourselves. The truth is I am not even hungry.

"I'll have a Coke," I say.

"I'll have the avocado and Muenster sandwich and a bottle of Miller," Mr. Howland says. He waits for me to say something. "Order something to eat; later, you'll be hungry."

I'm wishing we were at McDonald's because nothing here looks good.

"Can I have a grilled cheese?" I ask.

"What kind of cheese?"

"American cheese?" I say.

I know that this is a stupid order and that I look childish ordering American cheese, but I don't like other kinds of cheeses.

"I'll have a Miller, too," I say. "Forget the Coke."

The young vampire doesn't seem to care that I'm not old enough to have a beer. He crosses out the Coke and lets me have the beer.

"This is what we need to do more often," Mr. Howland says. "Get out in the world like normal people."

"That would be nice," I say.

I don't remind him of all the fun we had at the Happy Family Chinese Restaurant. The memory of our other lunch out in the world, the one in South Jersey, comes back to me almost in the form of a flashback. I see Tim standing outside my car with Mr. Howland, the two of them speaking so seriously to each other. I think back to the expression on Tim's face as they stood there, the expression I couldn't quite identify at the time. He was looking toward where I was sitting in the car by myself. He was talking to Mr. Howland, but he was looking at me. Now, from a different perspective, I would say he wanted to help me. Sitting there in the passenger seat of my car, I got a weird feeling that he might want to give me some advice on what to do next, maybe something along the lines of the Dracula Principle, but more useful for the future.

Our beers arrive, and we chink glasses.

"*Salut,*" Mr. Howland says, and drinks.

My beer tastes so bad I can barely swallow, but, I figure, like everything else I've really disliked in life, it will be better after a few more sips.

"Do you think people suspect us?" I ask. I'm trying to gauge how worried Mr. Howland is at this point. My sense is that people are well past the suspicion stage. We are now dealing with people who think they know the truth.

"I don't give a good god damn," he says.

He reaches across the table and holds my hand. He twirls my mini–Mr. Howland bracelet around on my wrist. I wish he would stop because there is something about being out in public, even if it is in a vampire bar with a junkie for a waiter, that makes me embarrassed about us. His dark, shadowed face and his hairy, fully developed arms and the gold caps on his teeth don't match with me. I only got my braces off two years ago, and my teeth haven't even had a chance to get all rotten yet. I slug the beer, hoping to quell the sensation of floating outside my body and out the door and over to wherever Barbie is with the other kids in my class. It works; I start to get a buzz. I feel like Emory must after he's had the third vodka and V8. He says "click," and we know that means that he's feeling pretty good.

"Click," I say, but Mr. Howland doesn't get it, so he doesn't say anything back to me.

Fortunately, Mr. Howland has to stop holding my hand when the food comes. My perfectly normal grilled cheese is on brown bread and is covered with sprouts and tomatoes, rendering it most unappetizing. I begin the process of picking off the sprouts and setting them in a pile on top of the tomatoes.

"You are hopeless," Mr. Howland says.

"Hey," I say, "did you really steal your wife from that guy Tim?"

"He's full of it," Mr. Howland says. "They were never more than friends."

Though we are sitting right across from each other, I feel about a million miles away from Mr. Howland. Fifteen years, the difference in our ages, might not sound like much when you think about numbers, but suddenly fifteen years of life seems like quite a long time.

"When we're married, I will teach you about how to eat healthy food," Mr. Howland says.

"You're already married," I say, noting the obvious.

"Not for long," Mr. Howland responds. He takes a long drink of beer.

"Listen," he says, "I need to tell you something, but I don't want you to freak out."

I start to think that maybe this is about Ms. Clewell, but it isn't.

"Melinda knows, because she was listening in the day I called about going to South Jersey. I've been trying to keep a lid on things, but last night she went crazy and threw all my stuff out the window, even my twelve-string guitar. I slept at Ron's."

My stomach falls through my body. I knew something like this was possible, likely even, but I feel like puking anyway. At this moment, if I could talk Mr. Howland out of getting divorced, if that is what he is really thinking of doing, I would do that. I imagine a conversation where I convince him that he and Melinda can work things out after all. I'll be going to college, and they can get back to their lives. In my imaginary conversation, I remind him about their house, a house they have put a lot of work into fixing. It's a pretty nice place, even if it does look like a house where Hansel and Gretel might get shoved into a potbellied stove. It occurs to me that Mr. Howland might actually believe that he and I are going to get married. Suddenly, everything seems ridiculous.

"Where will you live?" I ask.

"How about here in the city?" he says.

"Sounds good," I answer. "Maybe you could live in the

Empire State Building. Someone told me if you drop a penny off the roof, you can split a person's head open." I know I am talking nonsense, but I can't stop.

Mr. Howland glances around the dark restaurant. It's hard to know what he is thinking, but I bet it is something about how much he hates being a teacher and being married and how he wishes he lived in New York.

"What would Old Leather Head say if she could see us now?" he asks.

"Nothing good," I say, imagining that this is something my mother would have said if she were here.

"Hey," I tell him, "Confucius say, be careful of . . ." I put my hand over my mouth and mumble some fake words as we leave the restaurant.

Art Galleries

IN MY OPINION, we are walking too fast toward the art galleries. We still haven't seen a single person from our school. My guess is that they went to the movies or some other fun place and that they aren't getting dragged around to galleries. There are sunglasses spread across a blanket on the sidewalk, and I stop to examine them. Mr. Howland acts impatient, which makes me want to linger longer over the selection. I buy a pair of pink plastic glasses, sort of movie-star-like.

"That was a waste of money," Mr. Howland says.

"They were three dollars," I tell him. "I have forty-seven more dollars to spend as I please."

He doesn't respond.

"Furthermore," I add, "people will think I am a famous person traveling incognito."

Around Mr. Howland, I can use multisyllable words like "incognito," the very words that get me into trouble with anyone other than Patty.

There are large canvases with swirling, bright colors hung on ivory walls in the first gallery. Already I'm getting the feeling I've never told Dr. Chester about, that I've never told anyone about. It is a feeling I am going into another dimension where there is only emptiness and darkness and me. This feeling has gotten worse and more frequent since my mother left. I am floating in a soundless space without connection to anyone or anything. The best remedy is to fight back by being annoying to Mr. Howland. I tug at his shirt as he walks around; little does he know that his shirt is the only thing keeping me in this dimension, the anchor holding me on Earth.

"Stop pulling on me," he says.

"I am a blind person," I announce. I put on the pink sunglasses and continue to hold tightly to Mr. Howland's shirt.

"Let go," he says.

"I can't," I tell him. "I am a poor blind woman who wants to leave this place."

"You are insane," he says.

When we step back out into the street, I can let go of Mr.

Howland. I walk gingerly because I don't know how long the feeling of being okay will last.

"No more galleries," I protest.

Mr. Howland takes me into another gallery. This one isn't so bad because it isn't paintings; it is ordinary objects that are extra big. There is a big can of soup and a big crayon and other extra big things. Eventually, the idea gets boring, as you can probably imagine.

"Please," I repeat, "no more galleries."

Mr. Howland drags me down the street toward the next one. This gallery is more like the first. Flat gray carpets and ivory walls. The pictures are swirling lines again, this time sand-colored lines, giving the impression you are looking at layers of sand from underneath the ground. Mr. Howland likes these pictures. I sit down in a chair by the door while he walks around. He seems genuinely interested in art, and he seems genuinely surprised that I am not. As I am watching him and the few other people quietly appreciating what they see, it hits me that if I don't leave, I will enter the dark dimension and I will need to ask someone for help, not something I feel like doing.

My Escape from the Art Galleries

IT IS A BEAUTIFUL DAY OUTSIDE. I hurry away from the gallery toward the corner and I see Tyrone Love and the other outcast kids walking in a big group; for a minute, I think that maybe I could join them, but Mr. Howland would find me. So before they see me, I raise my arm in the air and a taxi pulls up and I climb inside. I'm still wearing the sunglasses, and though I haven't seen myself in them, my guess is that they look pretty good.

The taxi smells like some kind of scented oil, which makes my stomach heave, and the driver is sinister-looking.

"Central Park," I say.

The driver writes something down on a clipboard and pulls out onto the street. I really don't know where we are, and I don't know where Central Park is either, but he seems confident about the direction we are heading. I slump down as we pass Mr. Hurly and Tyrone. They are smiling and having a good time together. Maybe Tyrone appreciates art more than I do, despite our other similarities.

New York City is jam-packed with people going places in a hurry. There are people waiting to cross the street at every single corner.

"My mother is in the hospital," I announce for no apparent reason.

I don't even think the driver hears me because he doesn't respond or turn around or express compassion or anything at all. Or maybe he doesn't want to get involved in my problems. Maybe his own mother is sick and he doesn't want to dredge up any bad memories. Or it might be that he doesn't even really speak English. His name is about fifty letters long, some of which I don't even recognize as letters—they are more like mathematical symbols. He could be wondering about something important and not want to lose his train of thought.

"What entrance?" he asks.

"Any entrance is fine," I say. "Whatever is closest."

I realize this is a stupid answer and that I have just revealed I have no idea where I am going. He takes me up to Fifth Avenue and Sixty-fifth Street and stops near a gate that leads into the park. The ride costs seven dollars. I give him ten and get out because I can't do percentages, being terrible at both math and science.

I've only been to Central Park once before. My parents took me to the zoo when I was pretty small and I vaguely remember seeing a walrus swimming in a tank and I would like to see that walrus again. I enter the park through the stone gate, realizing I will never be able to find the zoo or anything else. This park is gigantic. I walk down the sidewalk. Everything around me is blooming—the leaves are opening and I think of a poem we read for English class. "Nature's first green is gold," the poem said, and I'm pretty surprised, because it actually is. The leaves are still so new that they aren't fully green yet. The sky is bright blue, and there are huge red tulips in patches growing up and out of the ground.

I make my way to a playground that has swings and a seesaw and monkey bars and even a makeshift tree house for kids to climb on. There are lots of children playing here, but I'm not sure how many brought their actual mothers because most of the women are black even though most of the kids are white. I sit down on a bench and point my face toward the sun. I'm tanning myself when a little girl in a denim jacket and jeans tugs on my hand.

"Hey," she says, "will you go on the seesaw with me?"

There is a black woman standing behind her who seems kind of depressed about being here. "Leave that girl alone," the woman scolds.

"No," I say. "It's okay. I'll go on the seesaw."

I follow the girl over to the seesaw. She climbs on one side and I climb on the other. Naturally, I don't put my entire weight on it because that wouldn't really be much fun. My side would be perpetually on the ground. I use my legs to push us up and down. She seems to be having a pretty good time. But it is hard work to keep us going without crashing.

"Okay," she yells, "that's enough."

She gets off her side, almost causing me to slam into the ground, but I catch myself.

"Do you like the monkey bars?" I ask her.

"Not much," she says. "I'm scared of climbing."

I walk over to the monkey bars and climb up to the highest rung, and then I sit there like I'm the king of the playground. My little friend is bugging her nanny to get on the seesaw again. There is a boy playing by himself in the sandbox. He's got a mini-bulldozer and a few trucks. He looks like he's in his own world. I'm going into my own world. I'm remembering a bookcase back in our old house. Right above the doors of the bookcase was a clock. It was a small gold clock, and I couldn't tell time yet so it always fascinated me to think about what the hands were pointing to. I knew that time was important because my favorite show, *Popeye*, came on at five o'clock. To tell the truth, I'm not sure that clock even told the correct time. Inside the bookshelf under the gold clock were my favorite books. For my birthday my mother gave me hologram editions of *The Little Mermaid*, *The Emperor's New Clothes*, and *Cinderella*. There were other books in that case I'd gotten too old for but still liked to read. My mother's favorite book to read to me was about a woman who sees a scarecrow one day and steals her clothes. She likes the outfit the scarecrow is wearing, so she takes it. After that, every night the scarecrow haunts her and keeps calling to her, "Give me back my clothes." When my mother read that line, she said those words in a spooky voice. Finally, after about a week of being haunted, the lady who stole the clothes is waiting for the scarecrow. As soon as the scarecrow says, "Give me back my clothes," the woman screams out from under her covers, "Take 'em!" That story knocked my mother out every single time. My mother wasn't the least bit sad when she read that story. She loved to yell "Take 'em!" and then start laughing.

My personal favorite was *Bread and Jam for Frances*. That was a book about a little bear who refused to eat anything other than bread and jam. She was completely stubborn. Finally, after holding out for almost the entire book, she gets tired of bread and jam. By the end, she is eating all kinds of crazy food.

As I look at that little boy with the bulldozer, some questions start to dawn on me. I realize I have been living my life like a detective, relying only on my powers of observation to find answers to questions that have bothered me for a long time. If the point of getting rid of Tommy was to make our family normal, why did my mother allow me to be so weird? Why did she let me drop out of nursery school? And why did she let me wear corduroy pants and a beaded Indian vest to school on dress-up Wednesdays in third grade when it was *normal* to wear a dress? That teacher even sent a note home, but my mother let me go on wearing that beaded vest and those corduroy pants every single Wednesday. If she wanted me to be like everyone else, why did she let me wear those clothes and quit nursery school so that I could stay home and play Monopoly with an invisible chipmunk named Sucan? If being normal is the point, why does my father allow Karl to live in the garage and sit right out in public on the steps of his office? It dawns on me that I may be a lousy detective.

Right then I decide I have to find my way to the hospital. I climb off the monkey bars and jog out the gate I came in and get another cab. This one isn't so interesting because now I am getting used to the whole thing. I tell the driver, another foreign guy, that I need to go to Memorial Sloan-Kettering Cancer Center.

The hospital is much closer than I thought it would be—only a few blocks. The driver drops me off, and I am alone in front of the building wondering why cancer has its own symbol, or at least I think it is a symbol of cancer that is hanging right next to the name of the hospital. It could just be the symbol of doctors and hospitals, but it makes me think of cancer and how everyone in that hospital has cancer. I focus on a man about my father's age walking out the front door who could potentially have just found out that he has cancer, or that he is getting over cancer—totally relieved he is cured or in remission and going out to celebrate with family and friends. He was probably scared shitless for the longest time about whether or not he was going to live or die, and then, ten minutes ago, the doctor could have said, "I have some very good news for you; you are going to live. The cancer is gone." The news would be cause for joyous celebration. Maybe he hasn't even told anyone yet. His plan could be to enjoy this moment alone for a few hours before letting everyone else who has been worrying for months and months know he is fine.

I am trying to figure this out as I get the courage to go inside the building, through the revolving door, which I finally do. Right away I start getting that stomachache I had in the car when my father tried to bring me to New York. I fight it because I don't want to have to puke or look sick because they could decide to test *me* for cancer and then discover that I've been dying for years without even knowing I was sick.

There are paintings hanging in the lobby, but they are not the kinds of paintings you are supposed to study the way Mr. Howland was studying the paintings in the galleries. These are colorful paintings, which are most likely meant to take your mind off of cancer. Despite the cheerful, fun pictures, my attention goes right to a woman sitting in a wheelchair who looks like she's going to live for about ten more minutes. She is basically a skeleton in a nightgown. There is a needle from an IV in her arm, but it can't be doing too much good. The people standing around her are probably her family, who brought her down to the lobby to see something other than her hospital room for a little while. She looks like she couldn't care less about seeing anything other than her bed. When I look carefully, I can see that she is younger than my mother, probably not much older than I am. The feelings of swirling, dark spaces are returning, so I head to the elevator without even knowing which floor I'm going to or what I'm going to do when I get there.

Inside the elevator there are signs up for people who want to attend support group meetings, both sick people and their families. I wonder if my father would ever want to be in a support group, but something makes me doubt it. He mostly doesn't like people and prefers to be alone. My mother might enjoy a support group, especially if they read a book and discussed it. I ride the elevator for a while reading the flyers before I realize I need to go back downstairs and ask someone where my mother is. I'm hoping the totally scary wheelchair woman will be gone when I get there, and luckily, she has been taken somewhere else. At the desk, they tell me that my mother is on the eleventh floor, pretty high up there.

Back on the elevator, I press the button, but it takes me three arrivals before I get off and actually start looking for her room. Most of the doors are only partially open, so I can't get a good look inside the rooms. Not that I want to see, but it is impossible not to try. Maybe the weird compulsion I feel is the suspicion that, if I look long enough, inside one of these rooms there will be something completely unexpected, something like a clown or a Harlem Globetrotter or a vampire, or anything other than people sitting around the beds of sick people they love. God himself could be inside one of these rooms explaining why he did this. I picture God as either a very old man or a little boy in overalls sitting there holding the hand of the woman in the wheelchair. He may be telling her it is okay to close her eyes.

My Mother's Room

I STAND OUTSIDE MY MOTHER'S ROOM in a trance. I'm biting my nails like mad, making them hurt and bleed. A nurse with a nice accent finally asks me if I need something, and without even answering her I pull open the door to my mother's room and step inside. There are two beds in the room, and my mother is on the right side. She is sleeping; her eyes are closed, and her mouth is slightly open. There is a curtain between her bed and the bed on the other side, where a person curled up in a ball is also sleeping. The room smells of sickness, but I think the sickness smell is coming from the other bed. I stand over my mother, staring at her exactly the way I used to when I had my recurring nightmare. It still works, and she wakes up and raises her eyebrows as if surprised to see me. She is very thin and very white, almost ghostly white. My mother reaches out for my hand.

"You came," she says. "I know you were afraid."

I'm confused as to why she isn't yelling at me and calling me selfish, the way everyone else is thinking I am selfish, the way Patty's mother glared at me when I told her that I hadn't been to the hospital to see my mother, not a nice look. But now my mother is looking at me like she feels sorry for me when she is the one who is sick and possibly dying.

"I made a Kippy burger," I tell her.

"Did she like it?" she asks.

"Well, she ate it."

"Did you wash the pan?"

I see my mother's mind working, wondering if I left the Mighty Dog–caked frying pan sitting in the sink for days on end. That is something I would do. In fact, it is something I *did* do, but I'm not going to confess to that.

"Yes," I lie, "I washed the pan."

She looks suspicious.

"How is tennis?" she asks.

"I won nine matches and lost six," I tell her. "I should have won eleven or twelve, but I messed up a few," I say.

"Do you need anything?" she asks. And then she realizes that I am here by myself. "How did you get here?"

"I'm on a class trip to see art galleries. I came for a visit."

"They gave me something for pain that makes me sleepy," she says. "Will you please come back when I can stay awake?"

Rather than grilling me about the details of my comings and goings, as she normally would, she closes her eyes and squeezes my hand. She looks exhausted, and her hand feels almost weightless, the way I feel weightless when I get worried.

I'm not ready to leave, but she is falling asleep. Her foot is sticking out from under her covers. Her leg is thin, and she looks so light that I feel like I could carry her around the room without any trouble. Like I could carry her out of this hospital and back to her own bed so Kippy could see that she is all right. I reach down and hold her foot, and I start thinking about Tommy, and where he might be—if he can come to visit our mother in his invisible angel form. Maybe he is here right now while she is sleeping and I'm holding her foot. I know she would have stayed awake if she could have; she is too tired. She just couldn't. I've got her foot though, her size nine and a half triple A foot that needs specially ordered shoes.

I sit on her bed for quite some time. Outside the window and down on the street somewhere in New York City is Mr. Howland, who is probably hemorrhaging with fear right now about losing me—about me escaping. I don't know what time it is, but I imagine the classes are most likely meeting at the bus right about now. He is probably pissed as hell at me. But I don't even care. Patty can sit next to him and hold hands with him the whole way back to school.

My mother is sound asleep, so I put her foot back under the covers. I kiss it before I do, which I know is a very weird thing to do. I know. I kiss the narrowest part on the bottom. I even press it against my cheek for a second, feeling glad that her roommate is behind a curtain and cannot see me. I will come back. That much I know. I say goodbye to Tommy and Sucan because I am pretty sure that they are both sitting in the chair next to the window—you'd probably say it was my imagination, but I can see Tommy next to Sucan wearing red overalls and a straw hat. Sucan is in a blue turtleneck sweater. It's been a long time since Sucan and I have seen each other, but he looks exactly the same. Tommy nods his head at me as if to say, I'm here and it's okay. If they could talk, I think they would both tell me that I'm not as bad as people think. After all, if my mother can forgive me, maybe I can forgive myself.

I get back to the lobby, and I don't wonder anymore about sick people and cancer because I have a bigger problem. I find a pay phone and make a collect call to my father, who accepts the charges, and I tell him that I am in New York and that I left my school trip and went to the hospital and that I missed the bus. He asks me how much money I have, and when I tell him he says I should take a taxi to Port Authority and then take a bus back to New Jersey. He makes it sound like it will be easy. He says he can't come get me because he has an important meeting and he needs to be in his office, but he will stay at his office until I get there. He asks about my mother, and I say that she is sleeping but okay. I tell him to call the school so that I don't get in trouble. If he tells them I went to see my mother, then I probably won't get in trouble. My mother remains the key to getting out of trouble these days.

Port Authority

PORT AUTHORITY IS A VERY BIG PLACE. When I finally find my way to the ticket area, which has about three hundred windows, there is a young guy who asks me to give him four dollars and fifty cents so that he can get home. I give him the money; a man next to me is staring at me like I'm an idiot, which I probably am. The people waiting in lines look like they have somewhere very important to go. I get my ticket, wondering why I didn't get a ticket to someplace far away and disappear. How am I supposed to face Mr. Howland? After being lost about five more times, I find my way to the bus and wait in line until we are boarding. It is amazing that being confused and busy has kept me from feeling like I am slipping into the other universe, the dark universe. The bus helps, too, because there are other people trapped in there with me; we are all in this together without really being together. No one expects anything from anyone. We have to trust the bus driver and the other people that everything will be okay. I like situations in which I have no control, situations where I can sit back and let someone else be in charge.

Before we get rolling, a lady gets on the bus and sits next to me, which really stinks because it was looking like I was going to have two whole seats to myself. The worst part is that she might be a nun or something. She has on a black dress with a big gold cross around her neck. She is older than my mother, and she is taking up a lot of space with a big bag that she could easily have put in the luggage rack above us. To be honest, nuns have always spooked me. I had a dream last summer about some priests and nuns riding on a wagon that was coming to take me away, presumably to either Hell or Limbo, and it was very scary. Fortunately, she's not acting like she wants to talk to me or anything. But as we pull out of the Lincoln Tunnel into New Jersey, I suddenly get talkative myself.

"I was wondering something," I begin. "Tell me if it is a stupid question, because it probably is a stupid question."

She looks at me and says that I can ask her a question.

"Do you know anything about Limbo?"

"Limbo is, I believe, the sort of halfway house for unbaptized souls," she says. She doesn't seem exactly sure, which worries me because you would think that a nun would be sure about something like Limbo.

"What do you think is the worst sin that a person can commit?" I ask her.

"I guess that would be a mortal sin," she says.

"Like murder," I say.

"Well," she says, "more like premeditated murder. I don't know about crimes of passion."

She is sitting there thinking about the questions, I can tell, but I'm starting to think that the black dress really is just a black dress and that she isn't a nun at all.

"Is there something special I should call you?" I ask her. "Do you go by Mother?"

"Why would I do that?" she asks, surprised by the question.

I feel like an idiot. Why in the hell did I think she was a nun? She must think I'm some kind of lunatic.

"I thought you were a nun," I tell her.

"Oh," she says, and laughs. "I got you with the cross."

"And the black clothes," I say. "Minus the veil."

"Have you done something wrong?" she asks.

"Well," I say, both relieved and disappointed that she isn't a nun. I simultaneously liked and feared the idea that, as a nun, she might have special powers of forgiveness. "I'm not exactly baptized and I didn't visit my mother in the hospital. I visited her now, but today was the first time." I leave out the stuff about Mr. Howland.

"If there is a God, I doubt he would actually send people to Limbo," she says.

"Kids used to tell me that Limbo was for people without limbs, and it did scare me, but I don't believe it anymore. I'm not exactly sure what I believe in terms of religion," I tell her.

"Faith is complicated," she says.

I keep waiting for her to try to convert me or something, but she doesn't seem the least bit interested in saving my soul.

"Do you believe in God?" I ask her.

"Yes," she says. "I do."

"That's pretty cool," I tell her. "I wish I did."

I want to ask her opinion on what happens to people after they die, but I'm not sure I'll get the kind of answer I'm looking for, so I don't.

I almost tell her that my mother might be dying, but I

check myself because I'm getting tired of people feeling sorry for me about that. I keep my mouth shut and watch the smoking and stinking refineries outside the window. I used to call it the inside-out world because it looks like a factory was turned inside out, exposing all the stuff you aren't supposed to see. I think that's why I've always liked this part of the turnpike, because the real stuff is right there and you know what you are getting. It isn't some glass building with a manicured lawn or a painting hanging on a cream-colored wall; it is the pipes and smoke and steam and fire. It is the truth, and I like that.

We finally exit the turnpike for the parkway, leaving behind the refineries and the other signs of industry. After a short stretch on the parkway, we get on Route 9 and make about four thousand stops. We don't miss one crappy town. I turn back to the woman next to me, who seems to have just woken up, and she says hello again.

"Were you asleep?" I ask her.

"I think so," she says. "Did we pass Lakewood?"

"No," I say.

"Are you still worried about Limbo?"

"Not so much," I tell her.

"Rotten things happen," she says. "No need to take it on yourself."

"I do that sometimes."

"I bet you do. Is your mother very sick?" she asks.

"Pretty sick," I say. "She slept through most of my visit."

"Well, I hope she feels better soon."

"Me, too."

By the time we finish our conversation, the bus is wheeling around the turn into the station.

"Nice meeting you," I say, though I realize that I didn't meet her.

"You, too," she says. "And don't worry so much."

"Okay," I say.

My Father

I GET OFF THE BUS thinking that I am glad to be away from New York City. It is a short walk to my father's law office, but I take my time because the sun is starting to go down and the colors are very beautiful. There is a chance that I am in deep trouble for running away, but on second thought, it probably doesn't matter to anyone after all. As I approach my father's office, I see Karl somewhat slumped over on the side steps and then I see my father standing on the porch. I suddenly get a terrible feeling that my worst fears are about to come true—visiting my mother has caused something terrible to happen to her. My dad waves his arm as if to call me over to him, and I realize if I go to him he might tell me something I can't hear right now. So I run. That is what I do. I run the other way about as fast as I can. My father is yelling my name, but I won't turn around. There is no way that I am going to turn around ever again.

I don't have a plan, but I do know that I intend to keep going no matter what. I turn down Cottage Street and run past the church where I didn't get baptized but that my parents took me to every now and then. I loop around back to Main Street and put my thumb out for a ride; despite the fact that I have never hitchhiked, I am not the least bit afraid of what could happen. A boy who looks maybe a year older than me pulls over in a wrecked-up Celica, a car as old as Mr. Howland's but not nearly as nicely kept. Also quite different from Mr. Howland is that the song playing on the tape deck is "Blinded by the Light," a song by the Boss himself off *Greetings from Asbury Park*. Normally a cautious person, I decide pretty quickly that this boy isn't going to drive me out to Goose Pond and murder me and chop me up in a million pieces and throw my parts into the swamp for kids to ice-skate on when the pond freezes. I would describe him as the boy version of me.

"Where are you going?" he asks.

Not having a destination in mind, I settle on the pharmacy. A freezing cold dose of Emory might not be the worst thing right now.

"Farmington," I tell him. "You know that strip mall where the pharmacy and the Cumberland Farms is? I work there and I'm late for my shift."

"I live up that way," he says.

This means that he must have money, even though he drives a wrecked-up beater. All the people who live in Farmington have money, whereas most of the people who live in my town don't have money. My father is one of the few people I know who has a lot of money. I wish I could show this kid my car so he could see how nice it is.

"Where do you work?" he asks.

"Farmington Pharmacy. Do you ever go there?"

"Not really," he says. "I think I've been in there once or twice with my mother."

"A lot of people's mothers go there," I say. I don't mention that Emory is having affairs with most of them.

The kid's face is pretty handsome, I must say. But he is too big for this car. He has to bend his neck to fit into the driver's seat. He is also extremely thin; his legs are skinnier than mine. He's wearing moccasins, and that is how I know for sure that he doesn't go to my school, because no one in my school wears anything other than work boots or sneakers, except for Mr. Howland, of course, who wears Italian loafers, or at least he says they are Italian loafers.

"Where do you go to school?" I ask.

"Christian Brothers," he says.

It occurs to me that he might be able to solve the mystery of Limbo if I ask him, but I don't feel like opening that can of worms again.

"What's your name?"

"John," he says.

"I'm Edna," I tell him.

"That's a weird name," he says. He doesn't say it meanly.

He says it like it's a name he hasn't heard much before. "It's sort of old-fashioned."

"I was named after my mother's best friend. She died in a car crash."

For most of the conversation we are sitting at a traffic light right in the center of town. It is somewhat awkward, more awkward when I tell him that I am named after a dead woman who wrapped her car around a tree. I'm worried that my father is going to start looking for me, so I make sure I'm slumped down in my seat. It won't be dark for a while yet.

"Believe me," I say, "I don't exactly love having an old-lady name."

John laughs a nice laugh that sounds like a snort. He has a really beautiful smile. His teeth are straight and white, like mine.

"Have you ever been to the Moon?" I'm wondering if I've ever seen this kid before.

"The Moon? Do you mean like space?"

"No," I say, "that place out by Goose Pond where people hang out. They just call it the Moon because it has craters."

"I don't think so," he says.

The funny part is I would have sworn that he was the kid looking at me that night at the Moon, the kid I snubbed.

"Where do you go to school?" John inquires.

I tell him.

"Wow," he says.

"What?"

"That's supposed to be a tough place. We played you guys in basketball, and after we beat you we had to be escorted out to the bus for our safety."

"That sounds about right," I say.

I don't tell him that Barbie and I volunteered to be the statisticians for the basketball team, and that we both used to enjoy watching our team start fights. It was the best part of the game. Every season we would go through a period when we weren't even allowed to have fans—only the teams, coaches, and the all-important statisticians could attend.

"Have you ever heard a song about a guy who is trying to save a prostitute named Roxanne?" I ask him.

"You mean that Police song?" he says.

"Is that who sings it?"

"Yeah," he says, "they're really good. The whole album is good."

I make a mental note to buy that album.

We get to the fancy strip mall in Farmington and he pulls up to the pharmacy door. I'm not really sure why I chose this as a destination, but I figure it is probably as good as anywhere, given the circumstances.

"Hey," he says, "I hope this doesn't sound weird, but are you dating anyone?"

I may be paranoid, but I think he is looking at my Mr. Howland bracelet.

"Why? Did you want to go out with me?"

I blurt the question out so fast that he almost misses it. It is an alarming moment for me, because I had no idea I was going to suggest that he take me out. On the one hand, it seems like a perfectly normal thing, but on the other hand, my life is feeling rather complicated and even this small interaction feels kind of scary. The weirdest part is that my eyes are welling up with tears.

"Actually, I was about to ask you to a movie next Friday," he says.

"Okay," I answer. "I could go to a movie."

"Do you want to give me your phone number or something?" he asks.

I'm wondering why this moment feels stranger than having sex with my art teacher; a simple request for a phone number from a pretty handsome guy seems like a normal teenage thing.

So I tell him my phone number and he tells me that he is going to call me. I jump out of the car like it is going to explode and run to the door of the pharmacy. When I look back, he's still sitting there and he waves at me. He continues to look pretty good, but I know my mind can change.

Work

IT IS A RELIEF to be where things seem like they always seem. Emory is smiling and talking to someone's mom over the pharmacy counter. Dale is doing a complex task that I probably never will master, and the temperature is slightly above freezing. I walk down the aisle where we stock the most expensive toothbrushes in the world. Emory sees me and gets a perplexed expression on his face. As I said before, his steady consumption of vodka and V8 doesn't keep him from staying on top of the schedule and other mundane things pretty well. In fact, other than his repeated car wrecks, there is very little sign that he is perpetually buzzed.

"What in the world are you doing here on a Friday night when you are not on the schedule?" Emory asks.

"Are you sure I'm not working?" I ask.

"Go have a look."

I walk into the office where Emory keeps the insulin refrigerator and I'm tempted to take out one of the brown medicine bottles filled with vodka, but I resist that urge and instead look up at the schedule that Mrs. Mooney, the assistant pharmacist, who I never see because she only works in the morning, makes each week. Naturally, my name is not on the schedule for today. I am surprised because I had almost convinced myself it would be there. It occurs to me I could write my name in since I don't feel like going home, but it would be obvious, because Mrs. Mooney's handwriting is about a thousand times neater than mine. Emory comes back while I am studying the schedule.

"What are you really doing here?" he asks.

Emory is exhibiting his spooky sixth sense about me. As I wonder what to say, I decide I would like to stay in the pharmacy for the rest of my life. Everything I would need to live is right here. There is water and milk and instant coffee and crackers and candy and cigarettes and all the Pepto-Bismol I could ever need in case of my stomach sickness. There is a stereo and a refrigerator and, for the times when I need a sense of accomplishment, the vacuum cleaner. There are vitamins and pens and paper and even tennis balls. What need would there be for me to leave?

"I am a fugitive," I tell Emory.

"Smiley, what in the good Lord's name are you talking about?" he asks.

"I ran away from my class trip."

"You did what?"

"I took off from New York without my class. I took the bus back, and then I hitchhiked here. I think my mother might have died."

I didn't expect myself to say that last part. But it is what I've been thinking since I saw my father looking so wrecked outside his office. Again I feel the tears coming on, and I stuff them back down my throat. It is clear that Emory doesn't have any idea what to say to me. Because I am not a woman he is trying to seduce and not one of his freakish family members, he doesn't know how to communicate with me. I'm supposed to be wisecracking Smiley, the girl with no problems. He looks at me with a serious expression.

"You could do me a favor," he says.

"Okay." I'm relieved that Emory has a task for me.

"Take these pills over to Button Up Milton on Main Street."

Emory calls the pharmacist in my town Button Up Milton because other than the fact that his name is Milton, he wears those old-fashioned pharmacy shoes with buttons on them, not the fancy suede bucks that Emory wears. He hands me a white paper bag with a note stapled to the top.

"Take my car," he says.

The thought of driving Emory's car isn't exactly appealing, but I don't have many options.

Outside, I examine the car. One of the headlights is smashed in, and the trunk lid is held down with a bungee cord. I climb in and sink into the plush red driver's seat. On the inside, it looks like a perfectly normal car. You'd never know how many accidents it had been in. I adjust the seat so that I can see over the large red dashboard.

This other pharmacy is only about ten minutes away. When I push the button for the radio, I figure that Elvis Presley is bound to be singing, but the radio is set to the same light FM station we listen to in the pharmacy. Exiting the parking lot, I go in the opposite direction from my destination, heading out toward the mall. As I approach Mr. Howland's house, I slow down. There are no cars behind me, so I can really crawl. Mrs. Howland's car is in the driveway, and there are still clothes scattered around below the upstairs window. I see a blue blazer hanging off an azalea bush. The glass on the picture of Paul Gauguin working in the bank is cracked down the front. There are some of Mr. Howland's drawings propped up against a willow tree. I think about taking the Paul Gauguin poster, but I resist when I remember the story my mother liked so much. I think about the trouble that woman got in for robbing the scarecrow, and my new goal is to try to avoid this kind of trouble as much as possible. Just for laughs, I pull farther into the Howlands' driveway, safe in the anonymity of Emory's death car. As I turn the car around, I yell "Take 'em!" as loud as I can out the window.

A few miles down the highway, I glance over at the graveyard that I've passed about a zillion times. My fear of death is great, and I have never once had the urge to enter a cemetery. But this time, I decide to look for my brother's grave.

I park Emory's car under a tree and begin wandering around. It is amazing how many dead people there are in this cemetery. I find a gravestone, a kid-size gravestone, but it is for a girl who died when she was a baby. She only lived about a week and didn't even have a name yet. As I wander, it dawns on me that I will never find my brother's grave; I don't even know if I am in the right graveyard. I sit down on a cool patch of new grass and watch some people putting flowers on a freshly dug plot. Normally, I'd get an attack of hypochondria or something in this situation, but I find myself feeling pretty good. There are flowers popping up through the ground all over the place.

When I get back into Emory's car, I open the sunroof and search the dial trying to find any Elvis Presley song I can. My car likes George Thorogood, and it seems to me Emory's car would want to hear some Elvis. I drop off the bag of pills with Button Up Milton and marvel at the seriousness of this other pharmacy. The official shoes and the official coat that Button Up Milton is wearing make me feel like I'm in a pharmacy from the past, the kind of pharmacy that existed before the 1960s, back when things seemed more organized and less chaotic. But even if Emory is the kind of guy who keeps vodka in the insulin refrigerator and puts shoe polish in his hair and jacks up prices and sleeps with customers, he seems a much better boss for me to have than Button Up Milton.

Driving back to Farmington, I look over at the graveyard where I stopped. None of the prayers I know seem right, so I make up an original prayer for my brother. Mainly, my prayer consists of picturing Tommy with his straw hat and his fishing rod in Heaven. The only words I use are to thank him for being there when I visited my mother.

At the pharmacy, Emory is in the office making himself a drink.

"Dale can drive you home," he says.

"No, he can't. Dale doesn't have a license," I say.

"I'll stick around and work if you want," I continue. "I'll vacuum. I'll even dust."

Emory must sense my desperation because he hands me a can of Endust and a rag and, shaking his head, returns to the drug counter. I carry my supplies to the gift area and look for something that needs dusting. In actuality, everything looks a bit dusty, so I begin with the statues. These statues are the kinds of things that you might see in a doctor's office or in someone's hospital room. My mother would never want one of these things in her hospital room, and I wonder if anyone in the world who was really sick and possibly dying would want a carved wooden statue of a nurse in a painted-on white minidress holding a sign that says, "Get well soon." But I dust her anyway because you never know. More interesting to dust are the big Smurfs. I tell you this, if I were in the hospital, I would much rather receive a giant-size Smurf, because Smurfs are blue and they are always cheerful, no matter what job they have. Even when Papa Smurf is working as a coal miner or a firefighter, he looks happy. Smurfland is a pretty happy place. After using practically the whole can of Endust on one shelf of Smurfs, I realize that I'm not doing such a great job. The Smurfs look too clean, almost glowing and sticky-looking. That is when Mr. Howland comes into the store wearing his Ray-Ban sunglasses even though it is now officially dark out. It is not clear how he knew I was here, but how many places could I be?

He, too, looks somewhat wrecked, but not in the same way my father did. He looks like he was recently shot out of a cannon and landed in the Farmington Pharmacy. I pretend not to see him and think about making a break for the back office. That plan presents immediate difficulty; it would require crawling down brightly lit aisles to avoid detection. I hold my ground. It doesn't take long for Mr. Howland to see me. He strolls over to me and lifts his sunglasses and stares at me.

"Have a happy Smurf," I say, and hand him one of the blue babies in a carriage.

"Why the hell did you do that?"

Spooky old Emory is looking right at us from behind the

pharmacy counter. He raises his Elvis Presley eyebrows as if to ask if I need help, but I shake my head at him.

"What?" I ask.

"Could you explain what you were thinking?" he asks.

"Baby Smurf says art galleries are boring," I say.

He keeps staring at me. It is hard to tell whether he is angry or genuinely confused.

"You really blew it," he says.

My sense is that this is in reference to the Dracula Principle. One of the key elements of the Dracula Principle is that you don't draw unnecessary attention to yourself. But Mr. Howland doesn't realize I don't want to rely on Dracula anymore. My mother's sickness has given me a kind of free pass to do whatever I want to do. I'm just tired of using it.

"Patty called your father, and he said he'd heard from you. Otherwise we'd still be sitting on the bus in SoHo waiting for you to come back. Doesn't that seem a tiny bit selfish to you?"

Mr. Howland's face looks extremely old, because he hasn't shaved and he has a reddish beard springing out of his cheeks. He is so much older than the boy in the car who wants to go on a date with me. His expression changes, and he remembers something.

"What is going on with Donna Clewell?" he asks.

"Who?" I ask.

"Is she one of your teachers?" he asks.

"She's my Latin teacher," I tell him.

"Why is she calling me and leaving me notes saying that she needs to talk with me? Has she talked to you?"

"Me?" I ask.

"Come with me," he says.

My sense is that if I go with him we will go to the Secret Spot and have sex. I am tired of his scratchy old face leaving my skin red and irritated. I glance at Emory, who isn't looking at us anymore. He is talking to Dale about some pharmacy-related issue.

"I need to keep dusting," I tell him. "I spent so much time in Smurfland that I haven't even gotten to these wooden doctors and nurses yet."

"Come on," he says. "Let's go."

"No," I say.

"Edna, don't do this," he says.

He says those words angrily. While it is a relief that someone is finally angry at me, I'm tired of Mr. Howland's anger about everything wrong in the world. I'm sick of being the one good thing in his otherwise rotten life. I can tell that he wants to fix this situation; he wants to make things with me the way they were. But for the second time that day, I walk away from him. This time I go straight to the back of the store with my empty can of Endust and hide behind Emory. Emory knows exactly how to act and sets up a big shield between me and Mr. Howland, who is still standing in the gift section looking pissed.

"Tell me when he's gone," I say.

"He's gone," Emory says.

"Are you sure?"

"All clear," he promises.

As I go to the phone in the office to dial my father's number, I wonder for a moment where Mr. Howland will go and what will happen to him. His clothes are hanging from bushes. If this were a movie, Ms. Clewell would be the character who opens the casket and sees Dracula sleeping in his coffin. As far as I know, Mr. Howland's mother is already dead, and depending on what Ms. Clewell intends to do, it is unlikely that he will get a free pass. As I am thinking, my father answers the phone and I tell him that I am at the pharmacy and can he come and pick me up. At this moment I appreciate Emory's lack of either nosiness or curiosity more than I can say. He lets me sit in the back room and doesn't ask me any questions at all. Mrs. Mooney has scheduled me for nine o'clock the next morning, a fact that would normally upset me, it being Saturday, but at the moment it feels sort of comforting to know that in the morning I will be back with the statues and the Smurfs and even with Emory himself.

After waiting several minutes, I wave goodbye to Dale and stand on the sidewalk in front of the store. This is not exactly the resolution for me, because I feel like something I've been trying not to think about is becoming something I can't avoid. My father's car is heading toward me and I wave. He pulls up next to the curb. He even opens the door for me. Inside, I don't know how to start the conversation. He leaves the parking lot without saying a word.

"Are you mad?" I ask.

"Should I be mad?"

"I think so," I say. "I did leave New York without anyone's permission."

"Well," he says.

"And then I ran away from you," I add.

"Your mother is worried," he says.

"Did you tell her?" I ask.

"Yes, I told her of your escapades," he says.

"Is she mad?"

The conversation is leading me to believe that my mother is not dead and that I badly misinterpreted my father's expression when I saw him outside his office.

"If you wanted to see her, why didn't you go with me?" my father asks. "Why did you make this so dramatic?"

My father is not big on drama. I would tell him *why* everything had to happen the way it did, but I see no point. I have learned that you don't necessarily need to tell everyone everything. My mother might get it, but my father would never see how a person could feel responsible for everything that happens in the world, even things that happened when she was practically a baby. My father is having another one of those mental conversations with himself. I look at the mole on his cheek, the mole that used to talk, and suspect that, while there is a certain resemblance, it was not my father climbing the stairs with me in the ghoul dream. Back then, I hadn't even *met* the ghoul from that dream.

When we get home, my father goes to his strange room

with his spooky creatures and I go up to my room with my big poster of Van Morrison and my collection of tennis trophies. I lie on my bed and close my eyes, and the next thing I know I am crying really hard, sobbing even, and I'm glad that my father is downstairs watching *G.I. Diary* with the sound up very loud because I wouldn't want anyone to see or hear me right now. But standing in the doorway is Kippy. She trots her furry gray self over to my bed and places her little paws on the edge of the mattress. I lift her up and touch her nose, which is cool and moist, another good sign. And although she does not give me kisses or consolation, she does curl up next to my leg and close her eyes.

As I lie there, it occurs to me that Mr. Howland was onto something with the Dracula Principle. It can take people a long time to see what is right in front of them. But, in the end, he was wrong. People do care about what's happening to you, even when you are certain they don't. They care about you even when you don't care about yourself. I wonder how I'm going to explain all this when people like Ms. Clewell and Patty's mom and even my mother start asking questions. I guess I'll have to tell them the truth; that it's all about the pipes and stinking smoke and lopsided mugs and broken posters of artists sitting in the bushes. Whether you like it or not, the truth can look pretty bad sometimes. Regardless of what happens to Mr. Howland, I think I'm ready to tell someone the whole story.

Sitting on my dresser is the sculpture Mr. Howland made of my body that I swiped on one of the days he was absent. I get off the bed and open the window, because the evening air is warm and I can smell the flowers that my father planted around the house. My first idea is to chuck my own body out the window and into the bushes below, but the sculpture would still be there, and in a sense, it's still my body. Instead, I take it over to the closet and put it on a shelf in the back. I'm going to keep it as a reminder of everything that happened. If Mr. Howland becomes famous, it might even be worth money someday. The bracelet is a different story. It is giving me a spooky feeling of wearing shackles, so I toss it out the window and try not to see where it lands.

Want to know another strange thing? Sometimes getting caught is the best thing that can happen to you. I'm going on a real date, and I might even start to like that kid John from Christian Brothers. And while I probably won't talk for a while about sex or about Mr. Howland and all that with Dr. Chester, I will talk, because whether you can tell or not, I feel better lately. If I'm lucky, I might even find out what and where Limbo is. I might even decide to get baptized, just to be on the safe side. Looking outside, I decide that even if none of it happens, the good stuff I am thinking about, my mother is still alive. And I am still alive. And despite the fact that my brother is not alive, I am pretty certain no one killed him. My father thinks my mother could come home soon, and even though her homecoming might end my life of free passes, the fact that she is alive and that she forgives me is more than I deserve. It could be the most beautiful thing in the world.